Meme McDonald's family is from Western Queensland. Meme writes books for children and adults. She has also worked as a theatre director, specialising in dramatic outdoor performance events. Meme's first book, *Put Your Whole Self In*, won the 1993 NSW State Literary Award for Non-fiction and the Braille and Talking Book Award. The animation of her second book, *The Way of the Birds*, was nominated for an AFI Award and won a best-film award at the Cinanima Festival in Portugal.

Boori Monty Pryor's family is from North Queensland. His mother's people are Kunggandji and his father is from the Birra-gubba Nation. Boori is a performer, storyteller and didjeridoo player. In 1993 he received an award for the Promotion of Indigenous Culture from the National Aboriginal Islander Observance Committee.

The first book Meme McDonald and Boori Pryor wrote together was *Maybe Tomorrow*, which was shortlisted for the 1999 Children's Book Council of Australia awards. *My Girragundji* (Winner of the 1999 Children's Book Council of Australia Award for Younger Readers) was followed by *The Binna Binna Man* (Winner of the Ethel Turner Prize for Young People's Literature, the Ethnic Affairs Commission Award, and Book of the Year in the 2000 NSW Premier's Literary Awards). Boori's narration of *My Girragundji* and *The Binna Binna Man* won the Australian Audio Book of the Year Award.

The main character in *Njunjul the Sun* is the same boy who has appeared in *My Girragundji* and *The Binna Binna Man*. He is now sixteen and, like all the characters in this book, is fictional.

Niunjul the Sun

Written by **Meme McDonald**
& Boori Monty Pryor

Photographs by Meme McDonald

ALLEN&UNWIN

First published in 2002

Allen & Unwin
83 Alexander Street
Crows Nest NSW 2065
Australia
Phone: (61 2) 8425 0100
Fax: (61 2) 9906 2218
Email: info@allenandunwin.com
Web: www.allenandunwin.com

National Library of Australia
Cataloguing-in-Publication entry:

McDonald, Meme, 1954–
Njunjul the sun.
ISBN 978 1 86508 641 5
1. Aborigines, Australian – Ethnic identity – Fiction.
2. Aborigines – Australian – Youth – Fiction.
I. Pryor, Boori, 1950– II. Title.
A823.3

Cover and text photographs by Meme McDonald
Cover design by Ruth Grüner
Photograph on page 79 by John Douglas
Frog illustration by Shane Nagle and Lillian Fourmile
Designed and set by Ruth Grüner
Printed in Australia by McPherson's Printing Group

5 7 9 10 8 6

for

Jai

for

Joe and Ciaran

for

Nicky Bidju and Paulani

with love and thanks

M.M. & B.M.P.

1

Our home's gone. Bulldozed. Bloke that owned it, sold it. Bloke that bought it, knocked it down. Another bloke cemented it up. Poured a big slab of concrete over our front yard, then over our back yard, then poured that cement over everything in between. Over all the nights round the fire laughing and shiakking, over the rose bush where my sister Chicky jumped out the window and landed on her butt, over that rickety old dunny out the back, over where that hairyman, that eunji, that ghost-fulla been choking m'sister and scaring the rest of us half to death with his yucky, wrinkly old hands. Concreted over all the teasings and fights and tears, over the headaches and heartaches and long, lazy nights.

Dingo Hire, that's what the sign says. Bloke hires out wild dingoes. Nah, only gammin', only pulling your leg! He hires out bulldozers!

Everything changed when our house went. Mum had to farm us older kids out with aunties and uncles. She only had room for the younger ones in that tiny little flat she found. Dad, he went off fruit-picking. He's been gone that long Mum reckons he turned into an echidna. Lost his way home.

I been living down with Aunty Milly, down there in Happy Valley. One of those places whitefullas put us mob when we were getting in the way of what they wanted to do. Called it a reserve or something. Said they were protecting us. As if!

Aunty reckons, 'What from? Our own land? Our 40,000 year old way of protecting our own selves?'

They got funny ways of naming things those white-fullas. Like opposite to what they're really thinking. My Aunty Milly laughs at that name, 'Happy' Valley. Like 'Happy', when they mean 'Real Sad Place'.

You see, Happy Valley is right next door to the cemetery. *Cement*-ery, get it? All cemented up? Real *dead*-ly place! That many of us mob buried over there, it feels like home, true. M'aunty, she always finds something to laugh about, but. 'If this place's "happy", next stop's gotta be a real good heaven!'

Me, I'm wondering why us Murri-fullas, us blackfullas, always talking about the next life. Waiting to die till we can find a place to be happy. I'm all for getting some of that happiness happening now. Right here, right now, like fully. Not in some way off maybe heaven.

She cooks the best flying fox stew, Aunty. Gravy and dough boys, um mmmmm, too deadly. Makes m'mouth water thinking about it. She taught us kids some bush ways, much as we were wanting to know. I lost my taste for knowing the old ways, but. I'm wanting what's new. What's exciting, what's out there on the other side of town.

That's what got me on this bus. This big, flash, air-conditioned coach heading straight out of town. A few other things gave me a bit of a push, but I'm not filling my head with that trouble now. I'm taking in the scenery whizzing by on the other side of this tinted glass.

First time I'm headed out on m'own. Except for footy matches and that. But then you're part of a team. The only team I belong to today is me.

I'm sitting up the back of the bus. I got m'new Wolverine shirt from m'mum. Got m'three in one – CD, tape deck, radio. An altogether too deadly sound machine! Going away present. Whole family put in. Got the receipt on me too. Mum said to hang onto that one real tight. Policeman pick you up for carrying a machine like this around. No way no bulleyman in blue's gonna take this one off me, but.

I'm singing up too. I Feel Good, da da da da da, like I knew that I would now, da da da da da. I got this deadly voice when I sing along with them old songs.

'James Brown, the Godfather of Soul, man.' That's what m'dad reckons.

See, we have karioki nights back home. Only us Murri's – that's what us blackfullas call ourselves up home – us Murris, we call them 'Murri-oki' nights.

My Aunty Gracelyn, she got her own machine. She sings that old one 'Crazy', that's her favourite, Patsy Cline. I'm thinking, don't worry about Patsy, it's m'aunty, she's the real crazy one. She's like a party happening twenty-four hours a day. You know Seven Eleven? Well, she's Seven Twenty-four!

I'm missing that mob. Like half of me got left behind.

Waving goodbye to Mum and the rest, they looked like strangers even before the bus pulled out.

I loved living with m'aunty. I love m'aunties, the whole mob of them. I love all m'family. But that living down there in Happy Valley made me sad. Real sad. And angry.

Getting on the bus, I didn't let that sad face get hold of me, but. I bit m'lip and waved them goodbye and pretended those tears running down little Chicky's face, and snuffling up my big sis's nose, and making my bro' look like he seen a car crash . . . I'm pretending all those tears are to let me know they love me to death. Not that they're letting me go for good. Those tears, they're holding me tight in their arms.

I'm looking up ahead, now. That road leading out of town's wide and straight and polished up new. My brand new nylon shirt's sticking into me. That don't matter. Bright blue, made in Taiwan, wherever that is. Wolverine plastered across the back. Air-conditioning turned up that cold it's giving me goose-bumps. Bus's full of migaloos, whitefullas, but who's worried? Nah, not me, I kid m'self. I'm a brand new flash-fulla heading off down the highway to the big city. And I've got a seat all my own. No bony little sister on m'knee. No mum or aunty squashing me up. No cus' teasing and that. No one but me.

Now I'm thinking of football, ice-cream, even the hairyman . . . anything to hold that mob of tears back from choking me up.

☼

I got a rich uncle, you see. Uncle Garth. He's a legend. He's done real well down there in the big smoke. That's what m'dad calls the city. Down there is different from up here. Uncle Garth's got himself a migaloo jalbu, a white-woman girlfriend, m'Aunty Emma. She's used to us mob. He's got his own flat. He's got a good job. He's got himself a car. And soon he got me. That's who I'm gonna be staying with. M'Uncle Garth and Aunty Emma.

I made sure I got m'self this good seat up the back of the bus. I wanna be seeing everyone else get on and off. Don't want everyone else gawking at me all the time.

And I wanna check out the chicky babes. No, true. Who doesn't? At least I'm honest. Better you be in the right position for checking out, than them catching you behind your back, picking your boogas, your nose, or scratching down there or something.

Jalbu down the front's got nice long curly red hair and a tight tank-top. Not that I'm looking that hard. Her mum's on guard, eye-balling any lookers. Like one of those circus trainers with the moustache, looking real nervous, worrying if their tiger might break out and do something real bad while everyone's watching.

I'm not looking that hard, neither, 'cause I still got Jody Butler on my mind. I saved up for a gold necklace and love-heart. Didn't nick it or nothing. She made me black, red and yellow beads for round my neck. We're tight as. Well, we were. But I been getting into trouble lately. Hanging out with my cus' Cedric and that. I didn't want her in trouble too. Didn't want me in trouble, neither, come to think of it.

I gotta sort myself out, see. This is my chance, going away down south to Uncle and Aunty's. M'mum reckons it's my last chance. But I couldn't tell her the whole story of what happened. You can't always do that with your mum and dad. You gotta protect them sometimes.

☼

Big bloke got on the bus where we stopped for lunch. Takes up the whole seat, mine as well. Don't know what he had for lunch but smells like we gonna be sharing it for the rest of the trip.

I'm thinking of calling out 'Apologise!'

Cedric called out in the middle of the movies one time. See, we got this thing going. If someone calls out 'apologise', you got to shoot your hand up real fast. Last to put their hand up, that means you're the one that did the boodgie, farted, see.

This time, just when the two lovers on the screen are kissing, Cedric yells out, 'Apologise!' The whole theatre shoots their hand up. Lollies, chips, ice-creams go flying all over the place. Everyone's that desperate not to be the last hand up and have the boodgie pinned on them.

The big bloke's munching on a packet of chips. Salt and vinegar. He offers me one. I can't resist.

'Where you headed, kid?'

No such thing as a free chip!

'Sydney.' I try and let it roll off my tongue like it's nothing special.

'Geez, you better watch your arse down there.'

I munch on m'chip. The big bloke keeps on about the crooks and the crime, the prostitutes and thieves and bashings down dark alleys.

'It's dog-eat-dog down there,' he growls. 'They'll eat you up. 'Specially you being black.'

I'm trying not to get those shivers up m'spine. I'm trying not to let him swamp me. I'm trying to look like I been there, done that, like fully. But he keeps at me like I'm some dumb myall, some bush Murri country-bumpkin knows nothing. Trouble is, he could be right.

'Yeah, lot of people in the cities reckon they wiped you lot out years ago. Lot of people where I come from out bush reckon they should've done a better job.'

I'm squashed up next to the window. Only thing I can see is darkness coming in all around. I can hear the big wheels going and the engine purring, but I can't see nothing whizzing past. We could be going nowhere. Or could be heading into outer space, to the stars and back. Or locked in a time-capsule buried deep in the earth. Or heading backwards at full speed. Or just going round and round in our own heads.

'Trouble is, you bastards aren't that easy to get rid of. You keep on bouncing back up. Which gets me to my next subject. You can hit, you lot. Over the years some of the best pugs in the business have been black. But now you got this young prancer dancer Anthony Mundine pretty boy always mouthing off about something. Should have stuck to playing Rugby League for St George. He should have shut his big mouth and done what he was told to do. They paid him big money, too, but he still whinged about not being picked in the State of Origin. So he spits the dummy. Reckons he didn't get picked 'cause he's black, so off he goes, sulking. I hate that. He was lucky to get given a guernsey in the first place. He should be grateful. Now he reckons he's the world's best boxer. What a joke! Out on the football field there's a lot of space and a lot of bodies. In the ring there's only two. You can run but you can't hide. All that black razzamatazz and fireworks he goes on with doesn't fool anybody. Let's see how far he gets when he comes up against someone that can hit.'

I'm wanting to argue back, to stick up for 'The Man' Mundine and the rest of us. I'm trying to find that warrior in me to stand up and be counted. I can't shape m'words or find the space between his, but. I'm feeling beaten and hopeless before I even get started.

'Look at Georgie Bracken, Lionel Rose . . . World class Aboriginal boxers. But could they handle it? Could they handle the fame and fortune? No way.'

I'm thinking, hang on, that's our legends he's talking about. That's not how it is.

'Mundine'll be the same. Hopeless. You buggers are hopeless, you know that? Money, booze, jobs . . . You can't handle any of it. Always goin' walkabout.'

I'm shutting down listening to him now. Mundine don't even touch grog or nothing so what is he talking about? I'm making that big-fulla stale-hamburger voice of his mix in with the sound of the wheels, disappear into a drone of sound that makes no more sense than tyres rubbing on tarmac.

I'm in no-man's land. I'm not back home no more. I'm not where I'm going. I'm out here copping whatever

comes. Thoughts come hurtling at me like meteors. I am the meteor as well as where the meteor is about to hit. Boy, is that cool, or what? That's deep. Didn't know I was so deadly!

You don't get yourself into trouble, I reckon. That fulla trouble, he just comes looking for you. He gets you by the scruff of the neck and says, 'Come with me, boy.'

I only did little stuff. Nicking cream buns from the tuckshop, that's not big time. I admit, when Cedric and I get together, we dare each other to do stuff. Seems safe when you're a gang of two or three. And anyway, everyone else's getting into trouble, not only us kids.

Down Happy Valley trouble is your way of life. There's that much pain and fighting got hold of everyone, I reckon they should call it Un-happy Valley. That pain soaks into you like rain, through your clothes, into your skin.

I gotta get that sadness out. If I don't get it out, there won't be any of me left to get. When I was a kid, mob of us used to collect big bags of those chonky apples, go look for wild plums over in the graveyard, make up our own feasts. We're bigger now, gone our own way, or locked up going someone else's way. Now those chonkys, they looking smaller and the trips fishing down the mouth of the Bohle and roaming around in the mangroves are getting less. My skin don't fit me no more. Everyway I'm pushing it only gets tighter. I'm not sure which way is up, true god. I gotta watch m'self. No mum or dad can keep you safe no more. No aunty or uncle can keep that trouble off your back.

See, I didn't have my bike helmet on. Didn't even own a helmet but I didn't tell the bulleyman police that. No way I wanna have them looking at me like a no-good Murri-fulla. Said I left m'helmut home. But they were looking for something else. They were looking to teach me a lesson. It was my turn.

I didn't backchat or nothing. But I was on my own, see. I'd had enough of hanging out and was heading home. Cedric and the others had gone into town for some action.

I could feel the bulleymen creeping up on me before I seen the car. Then they're there beside me. Nearly pushed me and my bike into the ditch. They're grabbing me and asking questions and shoving me into the back of the bulleymen's van, the black mariah, we call 'im.

I never been down the small house, the lock-up. I heard

about it, 'course. All us mob get a turn down there. It's Cedric's second home!

Bulleymen's story was that the school got trashed. I was near the school. So I get picked up. Them accusing me of something I didn't do don't worry me that much. I know it wasn't me that week. Next week it could be, but. I know that. They know that.

It's the other stuff I can't get off me, but. They took me down the police station, the lock-up, see. Us fullas call it the bulleymen shop or the small house. The big house is jail.

It's their eyes and their voices still got hold of me. The grabbing m'hair, bending m'neck back till it's gonna snap. They're grown fullas, big men, three of them. It don't take them long with a skinny fulla like me. You take a couple of punches from them and you're history. They try keeping you standing. Grab onto your clothes. M'clothes rip. I'm laying on the floor in a puddle. Wet m'self. I don't mind admitting it. Tell me you wouldn't, eh? Puddle of piss on the floor, crying like a baby, and they still not done with me.

They don't want to bust your bones, see. They want to muck with your head and your heart. They rough you up so's they can get inside you.

'You only half a nigger, anyway.'

'Your sister likes to . . . Your mother is a . . .'

I can't say that stuff. I can't say that stuff even to say

what they say. I'm chucking m'guts then, laying there on the cement floor. Feel like chucking m'guts now, thinking back on it. Only I got m'new blue Wolverine shirt on and it's a nice clean bus.

I can't get them out of m'head, but. That bulleymen stuff about what they done to your mum and your sisters. I know it's not true. It's the thought of it that eats into you, but, won't leave you alone. I can't get their eyes off me. They stare down at me, the three of them. Not one of them, see, not one wanted to help. They sat there watching. And I lay there like a baby, crying. I can't get those eyes off me. No matter how hard I scrub that soap into my skin.

They chucked me out of the lock-up and sent me home. Least I was out of that black hole. Sun's giving me a beating on my back. I'm not sure which way was home, neither. I was thinking, I can't tell m'mum. I got to protect her. She's had enough pain already. If m'dad hears of it, he'll be back here knocking on the bulleymen's door wanting a punch-up. Then I'd get m'dad chucked in the big house for assault. Locked away, not just gone fruit-picking. Murri-fullas locked up in that big house, they don't come out that often, unless it's in a coffin.

Used to be I had a frog that talked to me. Got me through. Like, I'm not wongy in the head or nothing. See, I had this pet frog, this girragundji. Got eaten by a snake. I could still hear my girragundji's voice inside me, but, real strong, telling me the way to look at things. A voice I could rely on. Now I can't remember when I last heard her talking. When I was laying there in that puddle in the lock-up, all I seen is darkness. No way no voice could live in there. Only darkness there for you when you fall this far down.

I was feeling sad and sorry for my black butt. Wondering which way's home. I got m'self back down Happy Valley. M'Aunty Milly, she didn't need no explaining from me. She knew. And she knew not to tell. Not this time. Not now.

I pissed blood for days. Don't know which hurt the most. M'kidneys or m'heart. They both been bleeding.

☼

I can't take no more. Cooped up in this bus, that big fulla's old-lunch and stale-after-shave's digging into me real bad, nagging at me till I want to vomit. Or maybe it's those bulleymen thoughts messing with me again.

He's taking up all his seat and spilling over into most of mine. I'm squashed against the window. The glass is cold on my cheek, hard on my head. We've come a long way south. It's the middle of the night. I try to push him off me. He's snoring up real big. Some people got that way of sleeping a nuclear bomb can't wrestle them out of it. I'm not wanting to take that sleep off him, neither, in case he starts up talking again.

One or two lights blink through the window like stars in the night. Then half-a-dozen together. Then a whole galaxy, a city. Brisbane. Thank the Lord – I'm aunty-talking now – I'm saved!

We pull into Roma Street Transit Station. He's gotta wake up now. Seems like he's only settling in deeper, but. I'm not waiting for him to shift. I clamber up and over, mountain-climbing my way out of that seat.

'Watch your arse, kid,' he barks down the aisle after me.

2

I'm sleep-walking. It's broad daylight here in this bus-station night. My eyes can't focus. Foreign beings, dazed, half-asleep, stare as blank as I feel. I see the image of someone, could be me, in a mirror. Looks like an alien space traveller. Maybe that's what you look like when the main part of you is still way back down the highway.

My body's on remote control. Finds its way to the gulmra, the dunny. I been busting since the sun went down but I couldn't get m'head around going to that gulmra on the bus. Hurtling down the highway, hundred ks an hour, sitting on a dunny? Good-go! For the rest of the trip your goona following you, sitting up in that cubicle beside you there, travelling un-deterred, 'under-turd'! Funny thought, eh?

I'm looking for a way out of this space station. I'm looking to fill my lungs with that night air, sweet with the smell of damp places. I walk out the sliding doors and into a half-night. Looks like it can't make up its mind. Not dark enough to see the stars, not light enough to see the green of grass or trees. A muddy kind of night. The air smells like it needs a good wash. Everyone's sucking on those plastic bottles just to get a simple drink of water. You gotta buy it packaged if you want it clean. These fullas are crazy.

I'm looking down at the bitumen. Somewhere under there is earth. Earth that smells like your mother. Warm and like it owns you.

What am I doing? I ask m'self.

I had to get out of the Valley. Where am I getting, but?

That's how it happens, eh? You think something and you think you're the only one thinking it. Like, after the bulleymen got hold of me, I'm thinking I gotta get out, right. I got to get somewhere I stand a chance to do something. I could feel m'self slipping into that same whirlpool that dragged m'cousin Sister Girl and all them others under. I'm thinking, I gotta keep m'head above water. I gotta be able to see the sun when it comes up and lay down safe when it goes down. You get out of that rhythm, you're gone. You get weak. Those bulleymen take you down to where there is no sun. Leave you so long in the shadows you forget the difference between living and dying.

And I was thinking, stuff school. What can they teach me? Stuff everyone getting drunk all the time. Even stuff Jody Butler. After the bulleymen got me, I didn't even want to go near Jody. She seemed too whole, too together. I was a mess of broken pieces. I stopped going to school, stopped hanging out, stopped everything, except maybe breathing. Just lay down there in Un-happy Valley, rolling things round in m'mind each day.

'You get out or you die.' It was like some voice telling me. I didn't know who or where that thought came from. But it was the only one left floating loose. The rest of my thoughts were tied up into a tight ball, hard as rock.

I didn't know how to get out, but. Most days I was just waiting to die. Thinking I was a no-good blackfulla. Garbage dumped on the edge of town.

I was thinking real sorry thoughts, and thinking I'm the only one thinking them. But sure enough, someone else was thinking my thoughts. M'aunty, she got hold of those thoughts. Aunty Milly, she musta reckoned she gotta do something to get me out or there'll be none of me left to get, like fully.

'Cause next thing I know it's happening. Aunty must have talked to m'sis, the oldest one, that got talking to the next one down, that got talking to m'mum that got hold of Uncle Garth and Aunty Em down Sydney.

This ticket arrived at m'mum's place. Bus ticket. M'sis brought it down here. I remember her walking over from the car. I knew she had something big to tell us. Probably someone died, I was thinking. She held this ticket out to me, just like that. Just held it there above the mattress I was camped on. I'm looking up and thinking what the hell is this?

'You got a ticket to Sydney.'

It doesn't sink in for a bit. I'm still trying to figure out if she's happy for me, or gooli-up, angry it isn't her going, or what.

Sydney, I'm thinking, like the word's got no meaning stuck to it.

Then it struck me like a lightning bolt. I'm staring at that ticket, shiny cover, printed with my name on it, mine to hold, mine . . . I can't take m'eyes off it. That lightning energy kicks in, m'heart's thumping, my mind's starting to unwind, the hard rock beginning to move, threads breaking free, possibilities, silly things that make me laugh opening out . . . A bus ticket to Sydney!

Now I'm thinking basketball. Uncle Garth knows all there is to know about basketball. Maybe he could show me a few moves . . . Maybe I could be a star . . . I'm a long lanky thing and when I set my eye on that hoop, it stays set.

Then I'm dreaming of me making heaps of money and sending half of it, maybe more, up home each week for Mum, for Aunty, for all the kids . . . I'm dreaming and I'm laughing and I'm feeling the sun shining in my face.

Aunty Milly, she sits me down and gives me a good talking to. Sometimes, when I look in her face, I'm thinking she's the last of how it was. She's my foothold back to those old times. She's living down Happy Valley 'cause it's the closest she can get to living bush. Not like most fullas down here now, living like they're refugees.

All the family, they worked hard to give me this chance, Aunty's telling me. Saved and put in their money when there's not that much to put. They fought to stay alive themselves so things would be better for us kids.

And she ended up saying about bulleymen, they not all bad. *As if!* I'm thinking. She's onto me, but.

'You gotta remember that.'

And I'm knowing she knows they busted me up. Secrets are safe with her, but. She got ones go back 40,000 years, she gotta be able to keep a secret goes back only a month or so.

She's a churchy one, Aunty. Full of forgiveness.

'There's good and bad in any place, in anyone, good and bad in all cultures. No uniform's going to change that. No colour of your skin gonna change what's in your heart.'

She's real serious.

'You one of our warriors, young fulla. You remember that. We need you. But first you go some place else, till you strong enough for back here.'

Tears are pushing up. She must have seen them 'cause we got laughing then. She seen the warrior in me. She teaching me how to hold those tears. She got me remembering the day the bulleymen pulled us up. Ages ago.

See, one time Aunty had a car full of us kids and that engine he cut out. Stopped dead. She's turning that key till her hand's ready to drop off. No go. That old bomb of a car's all puffed out. Not gonna budge for no one.

Aunty's telling us, 'Well, you kids, looks like it's Foot Falcon from here on. That ef'in' car's gone to God. Gave up the ghost.'

But then these bulleymen pull up beside us. We're gone, Aunty's thinking. She been using a couple of stronger words than that under her breath. She's praying too. I heard her. 'Dear Lord, shine down upon us today. For a wretched soul like me. Please, God?'

Two big blokes, that blue uniform all neat and clean, stride up to the side of the car. Aunty looks up at them, her eyes gone big and round, still praying. Us kids are shrinking down in the back, trying to look see-through. Bulleymen talk to m'aunty like she's a kid in Grade One. Give her a warning about seat belts and the maximum number of passengers it's safe to carry in a moving vehicle.

I was about to say, 'This vehicle's not moving.' I didn't want to get m'aunty into trouble with my smart talk, but.

Aunty keeps looking down at her lap, all humble. 'Yes officers. Thanks officers, sirs.' All polite.

They keep on real serious. 'Remember then. Five is the maximum. Not fifteen.'

Those fullas hardly made it back to their car before Aunty's calling out, 'Eh, bulleymen!' Real loud too. Then, 'Eh, look-out!' She surprised herself.

When they looked around she changed into her best

voice, real lady-like now. 'Excuse me, officers, sirs. I don't want to be of trouble to you but do you think you could possibly lend us a hand, please and many thank yous?'

I reckon she's thinking God been on her side so she should make the most of it.

The officers looked surprised. 'With what?' They stand there gawking.

Us kids're staring up big now, eyes nearly popping out, not game to let out a giggle.

'Could you, sirs, please give our car a little push to maybe help kick-start 'im?'

You know what? They did. True god. Like fully. They musta reckoned they couldn't *not* give us a push. All they seen was this real proper lady in a tight spot, just happened to be black.

Those two bulleymen got behind us, pushing our old bomb up the road. That bomb, she felt those bulleymen hands on her moyu, her behind. She got such a fright she kicked over first up, revved herself stupid, and took off like a getaway car at the scene of a crime. Never missed a beat till she got us back home down Happy Valley.

Aunty was praising the Lord the whole way. And our mob's great Creators as well. And praising up us kids for staying so quiet. We had no choice, but. We got the breath sucked right out of us by the sight of two bulleymen pushing our beat-up blackfulla car up the road, all us inside.

Aunty was even praising up the old bomb she'd been cursing just before.

'Remember how you couldn't turn her off, Aunty? That old bomb thinking she's so deadly, so full of herself, she wanna keep on cruisin', eh?'

My aunty's laughing up good.

'And remember,' she said, settling back all quiet now. 'Remember us when you go down that big smoke, that Sydney there. Never forget where you come from. Never be shame. 'Cause me, I'll be watching you. Every time I look up into that sky, I'll be watching for you there, remember that.'

I'm quiet now. Wondering what she meant. I'm not about to be asking. Those old fullas, they give you messages like that. Not for the asking about, but for the knowing when the time comes. I'm wondering about me in the sky. I'm wondering about what lies ahead.

Some fulla's mumbling something over the Transit Centre loudspeaker. Don't know what language but sure isn't Murri. More like mumble-fulla language. No way I'm getting left behind here in outer space, but. I sit watching, waiting for the bus door to open. Half hour later I'm still watching, ready and waiting. I'm not that hungry. My belly's still full of stale hamburger and after-shave.

The door opens. Praise the Lord! – I'm thinking aunty-talk again.

I hang back. Checking to see if there's any sign of the big bloke. Maybe I could get m'self a different seat. Everyone's got on. There's only me left. Big hamburger fulla must have got off and stayed off. The bus driver looks like he'd be as happy to close the door in m'face. I rush on.

I smile at the ginger-hair tank-top jalbu. She looks like she wouldn't mind coming up the back. No way her tiger-taming mum's gonna let her, but.

I double check. No big fulla in sight, but. My luck has turned. I'm spreading m'self out, settling in, tuning into a local station playing my kind of music.

Engine's turning over, purring like a panther. Door's closing. I'm feeling good.

Then I see her, a flying fox rushing for the door. Long black cape slipping through in the nick of time. The starched white around her face digging in tight. She's puffing and panting and can't find her ticket. Driver smirks and waves her through.

'If we can't trust you, Sister, who can we trust, eh? Show me your ticket next stop.'

He waits till she finds a seat.

Oh, no. No way. She couldn't.

She is. She's got her eye on the seat next to me.

There's other seats, I'm sure of it. Hell. Oh no, I can't say that. Can't she see? I'm trouble. I'm a smart-mouthed punk no-good Murri-fulla with a bad attitude.

Slowly, nodding at all the sinners down the aisle, she makes her way up the back, smiling.

That's not right, but. Nuns don't sit up the back. They gotta be down the front. Unless she's thinking of saving m'soul. Hell! I mean heavens! I mean, no-way, this is no-fair.

She sits down. Next to me. Smiling. That holy-water smell riding on every breath she takes. Goodness shining out of her like the morning sun.

Sweat starts up under m'arms, m'hands, across m'forehead. I close m'eyes so I don't have to smile back or do something nasty. Maybe she thinks I'm praying. Maybe I'll fall asleep . . . or wake up . . . or fall . . . I am falling . . . asleep . . . and I hear a voice . . . distant . . . laughing at me, real loud, but a long way off . . . like a voice I used to know. Maybe it's her . . . she's still with me. The nun?

'No! It's me. Your girragundji. You-fulla going to be okay. You're safe.'

I'm dreaming of the sea . . . of nuns blown along the beach like tumbleweed . . . of m'aunty . . . m'aunty and the nun . . . m'aunty the nun . . . of me riding on the back of a turtle . . . laughing . . . my heart light . . . soaring high . . . the sun . . . I'm dreaming of the sun . . . my girragundji's voice back with me . . . unafraid . . . talking to me . . . telling me things in language . . . same way them old people speak . . . that language I'm not knowing yet . . .

I wake up in a panic. In a hot and cold sweat. That dream turned around on me. Got tangled up in my nightmare. There were big fullas after me. Rubbing my face in . . . I don't know who's what or where I am. I'm trying to wipe it off m'face. Wipe m'self clean. I can't.

I feel a gentle hand on my arm, soothing, calming, like my mum's. But it's not m'mum's. It's her's. The nun's.

I try not to shrug her off. I'm shame as, but. Maybe I was yelling out, trying to punch the bastards.

I stare out the window, looking for m'self. All I can see is a reflection. Big martian eyes, long lanky kid, curly black hair, but nothing else that says it's me. And a shadowy figure behind, a nurse in an operating theatre, or a guardian angel. Maybe I died sometime back there. I could be living in the afterlife!

The nun, she offers me a Life-saver. I stare at the torn paper, the sweet pink musks. I could do with something to suck. Something that'll connect me with m'self.

There'll be a price, but. And I'm not wanting to pay.

I give in and take it.

'Where you from?'

See! She got me. Sucked in again. That sweet pink musk turns sour as.

I'm about to tell her I'm from Harlem, New friggin'

York, but I look in her eyes and I see that aunty-look and the words choose themselves. I tell her the truth. Before I know it, we're chatting up big. She knows half my mob. All those fullas that live down round Sandgate and that. She keeps on about one fulla there, must be an uncle of mine. I got that many uncles. I heard of him, but she knows a whole lot more than I ever heard. The way she's talking up about us mob, I feel real deadly just to be related.

Then her eyes glass over, all teary. The end of her nose pinks up and starts to run. I'm wanting to help her out but I don't have a hanky or tissue or nothing. I'm thinking of anything to get her mind off whatever it's got itself stuck on that's making her sad.

I'm asking her if she knows how the emu got its name. It's an old joke my uncle used to tell. Reckon it's worth giving it a go. She's looking at me blank. Just at the right time, someone walks past in the aisle.

I point and say, 'You know what us mob call that?'

She looks where I'm pointing and all she sees is the back of the person walking past.

She looks confused. 'A person?'

'No! His moyu. That's what we call that one, that backside, bottom, bum . . . moyu . . .' I sound it out for her. 'Moo-you.'

'Mooyou.' She sort of gets it right. 'What's that got to do with emus?' she giggles.

Got her! That first giggle flows out without her noticing, like water trickling over rocks way below a forest of trees.

'Listen up and I'll tell you.'

She wipes her tears on the back of her veil.

'Not so long ago, what do you call them fullas that write down stuff about us, you know, whitefullas that write books about blackfullas and . . .'

'You mean anthropologists?'

'Yeah, that's him. Well, this anthro . . . opolo . . . One of those fullas was up there studying our mob. Writing down the names of plants . . .'

'A botanist,' she butts in, nearly knocking me off my story track.

'Nah, that other kind of fulla, that anthro one. See, he's trying to cotton onto how we were talking and our language. Anyway, one time there, us mob was having a big dance, all painted up and that. He asked about the patterns on our bodies, the designs and what they mean. He was scribbling all this stuff down. Us mob was dancing up all over the place.

'He had this old fulla sitting down next to him asking him to tell him what was what.

'"What are they doing there?" he asked, pointing at the dancers.

'Old fulla looked up at him and said, "They been doing Hunting Kangaroo Dance."

'The bloke scribbled it down. After a few moments he

looked up again and asked, "What's happening now?"

'"He been doing Goanna Dance now. He been go down waterhole, look for dat snake dere."

'The anthra . . . anthropo . . . that fulla, he scribbled it all down. He scribbled and scribbled, getting down everything the old man said.

'When he looked up this time, one of the dancers was doing the Emu Dance. He was pecking the ground, facing away from that writing-down-fulla. His backside's sticking up. When that whitefulla looked over, he pointed at that dancer doing the Emu Dance, he pointed straight at him and said, "And what do you call that?"

'Old fulla, he looked up where that fulla was pointing and he was real shame. "Eh? Dere?" He whispered, "Dat's 'e moyu."

'The whitefulla looked again and said, "What?"

'"Dat's 'e moyu." The old fulla was embarrassed.

'And that anthro-opo-ist wrote down, "e-mu-u". Emu. And that's how that emu got its name!'

I'm raising one cheek off the seat, slapping my butt. She's choking, those tears flooding down again. This time it's from too much laughing. I better go easy on this one with the jokes, I'm thinking. She might pass out.

But then, soon as she's recovered, she's onto telling me one of her own. The one about what the bishop said to the nun. I didn't think nuns were meant to tell jokes like that, but.

I'm laughing m'self stupid. I tell her another one, one of m'best. Then she's got one better. We keep on, laughing into the dawn. Us two, me and the nun, we're out there in space, free of time and place.

Then the big city of Sydney reaches out its arms to us. Where we've been was way past any streets and buildings. In bits and pieces that city takes shape along the side of the freeway, our bus gleaming silver in reflections.

She's never been to Sydney, neither. She's heard it's a beautiful place. Sydney Harbour Bridge, the Opera House, Olympics and everyone friendly and that.

We go quiet waiting for that beauty to come and get us.

Now we're underground, burrowing through a tunnel they built right under the city. Disappearing into the belly of the big beast. I'm not game to look at her or take my eyes off outside. I'm wondering how they're keeping up that river overhead. Only little shower tiles on that tunnel wall. Something seems not right to me. I'm holding m'breath.

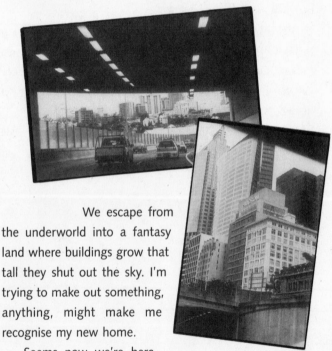

We escape from the underworld into a fantasy land where buildings grow that tall they shut out the sky. I'm trying to make out something, anything, might make me recognise my new home.

Seems now we're here, me and her, neither of us is that sure we should have left where we was. I can feel her same as me, unsure. I'm not about to hold her hand or touch her or nothing. But I'm wanting to give her something to make her strong. I tell her what Aunty Milly told me. 'Sometimes you gotta go away from where you wanna be, just so you can get strong enough to go back there.' Her eyes look real serious, staring at me. I don't know if I made it worse, or said something wrong, blasphemed, or she's about to hug me or burst out crying or what.

'Yes,' she says, real solemn, like she's running through the Rosary with her Hail Marys, Praise the Lord. Now she's looking at me like I *am* the Lord, Father, Son and Holy Ghost all in one, or good as. She keeps on saying to herself, 'yes . . . yes . . . yes,' nodding her head.

I always knew Aunty was powerful. I didn't know that power worked on migaloo ones, but. Nuns and all.

3

I got a scrap of paper in one hand with a phone number on it, my port, m'bag in the other, m'too deadly sound machine tucked under my arm, and me in the middle, ready to step out and take on the big city. Sydney, here I am.

Trouble is I got no uncle and aunty running up and claiming me. I'm feeling like lost baggage. The scrap of paper's getting that scrunched I can hardly read the numbers. They're just numbers all in a row. Don't match up with any image in my brain that says 'here's your new home'. Could be long way, could be close, could be they live anywhere out there. How far does out there go?

Never thought of it when I got on the bus days ago, but now I'm standing here, I don't recognise no one. There's people rushing all directions. I don't know none of them. Nowhere in the movies looks this lonely.

I'm wishing I hadn't said goodbye to the nun and told her 'course I'd be right. She was looking back at me and waving all the way out onto the street. Last I seen of her she had a nun either side of her carrying her bags like bodyguards or wardens or something. And her, she's turning back, waving over her shoulder, not wanting to let go. And me, I'm standing watching, knowing I'm the last image she has to remind her of what she's left. Then she smudged into a patch of light. Gone. Vanished.

People keep looking at me like they never seen a Murri-fulla before. They wanna look right into you. Right into your face and through your eyes, friendly and that, but. Migaloos don't do that up home. They know us Murris. We know them. We keep to our own places.

Maybe they been thinking they seen me somewhere before. Like I'm a footballer come down to play AFL. Sydney Swans. Or Rugby League. South Sydney. They could be mistaking me for 'The Man' Mundine, deadly eh? Don't mind them thinking that. They won't be picking on me if they think I can hit. Bet no one's got me spotted as the basketball legend I'm gonna be, the next Michael Jordan for the Chicago Bulls. Not yet. That's 'cause I haven't got the gear. The basketball boots, the baggy shorts, the singlet. M'Wolverine's as cool as but it don't say 'legend'.

My mind's gone all wongy now, stupid, making up thoughts so as that worry don't rush in and drown me. Pretending I'm a legend not a loser keeps that gnawing in my belly quiet.

Eh, look-out! Here they come. Aunty Em's rushing at me like she's busting a world record. Now she's hugging and saying sorry they're late and hoping I wasn't worried and there was lots of traffic and they couldn't get a park . . .

'Nah, no matter,' I take that worry off her before she's gonna pass out. When I first met Aunty Em back home, I been nicknaming her Rush Hour. Rushing here and there, always gotta be on time. She still got that pace about her.

Uncle Garth's sauntering up, grinning. 'Hey, youngfulla. You knew we'd get here, eh? Murri-time.'

We laugh up big and hug.

'Yeah, Murri-time, eh?' I'm sighing with relief, forgetting I was ever worried.

☼

Uncle Garth's got a powder-blue Merc. True god. Powder-blue, 280S Automatic. Real leather seats. Slides your butt all over the place round the corners. Maybe rich people got some special way of holding onto those seats, like suction butts or something. No wonder they walk all funny!

Me, I go flying across from one side of the car to the other every corner. Whole back seat to m'self. I get to see both sides of the city still heading in the one direction, like fully.

There's nowhere to park the Merc outside their place. Uncle's cursing. Reckons Bondi's getting too busy. I'm cursing, same, backing up m'uncle. Inside, I'm excited as hell to be here, to be where it's happening, the busier the better.

The front of their block of flats is all trashed. Graffiti, rubbish chucked about by passers-by. No one uses the front gate so it's rusted shut. You can see from the tracks, most people walk through the corner where the brick fence's busted up and fallen down. I'm thinking it's more like home than the flash place I got in my mind. We climb up the stairs. Uncle says something about the bullet holes in the wall. Some fulla come in and shot at some other fulla for drugs or something.

I'm thinking about the big bloke in the bus and watching m'arse. I'm thinking about the nun and Sydney Harbour Bridge and the Opera House and friendly faces. I'm still waiting for that beauty to come and get me.

☼

Aunty Em cooks up a big dinner for us. Reckons it's to welcome me to Sydney. Stir fry in the wog.

'Wog?' I'm going. Didn't know m'aunty would call those foreign-fullas that.

Uncle sets me straight. 'Wok. This thing, this frying pan here, you call 'im "wok".'

We sit around the table, no telly, just yarning. Aunty's onto planning the next day. Uncle's onto eating his dinner. I'm onto anything that's going. I'm tingling all over with newness, like that snake must feel when he sheds his old skin and struts his stuff for the first time in his new coat. I'm looking and touching and tasting everything.

Aunty's a school teacher, see. She's talking up about

the special kind of school she teaches at. Kids come from all over the place, all over the world, all different languages and that. Next thing, she's talking about me going with her, me going to school. Those brakes slam on real fast in my head. I'm onto anything but going backwards. I never planned to be coming down here to go back to school.

I look at Uncle for help. He keeps on eating and smiling and saying something about I might need a sleep-in tomorrow. I'm nodding and trying to get it across that I've done with school. I'm not sure that they get my message, but. I'm not wanting to be throwing my weight around on the first night, neither. Not that much of it to throw, weight that is, but I can dig m'heels in when I want. I might be a skinny fulla but I can G-O as good as.

Uncle and I get stuck into the clearing up and washing dishes. Aunty's got some work to do correcting before I go to bed. See, I got the sofa-bed in her study. How cool is that? My Aunty Em's got a study, like office, like important person. Books and filing cabinets and stuff everywhere.

Uncle's frothing up the suds.

'You still going for Chicago Bulls?' I been busting to get yarning about basketball.

'Lakers. I given up the Bulls. I'm following the coach now. Stuff the players. Those fullas are just into money, money, money, must be funny . . . Eh, look-out, sounds like Abba!'

See, I reckon I take after m'uncle. We got that same deadly sense of humour.

'No, Phil Jackson's the man. The Zen master of basketball.'

Uncle's favourite topic is the NBA – the National Basketball Association. You get him talking about those dudes over in America, he won't pull up for days. And I'm soaking it in. I can feel I'm starting my journey right here in the kitchen, wiping dishes with m'uncle.

Basketball was always better when he was a kid.

'We played on bitumen courts. I'd play till m'toes'd pop out and there were big holes in m'soles from all the lay-ups we were doing. Toes'd be pouring blood but we'd play on. You'd save for weeks before you could buy a repair kit and patch 'im up, glue a new sole on and sand 'im down. Eventually the hole would get that big it was beyond repair. Cardboard was the only thing that would work then. You'd have two or three cardboard cut-outs waiting on the sideline. Every time one'd get soaked with your blood and sweat you'd call time-out and reload your sole.'

As if, I'm thinking. In your Dreamtime! M'uncle's real good at telling stories.

'You watched basketballers back then. They played for the love of it. Since Jordan retired the game hasn't been the same. These young kids, they're all great athletes but their hearts are somewhere else. They're gifted, but their minds are on the money not the ball.

'These dudes do all this fancy stuff but most times when they shoot the ball they're shooting bricks. They forget the basics. They walk out on the court and leave the basics back in the change-rooms in the mouths of their coaches.

'You gotta remember the basics m'boy. Not just in basketball. But in life. Basketball is life.'

We finish the dishes. He wipes the bench that clean you can see yourself in it. He likes checking himself out, m'uncle. Gives him a good excuse, wiping those benches.

On the way to bed, Uncle slips me ten bucks. 'In case you need something and I'm not about,' he reckons. I reckon he just likes having me around.

'Get your dot into gear by the weekend and I'll take you down the courts.'

I suppose that's his way of saying goodnight and he loves me.

☼

I'm laying here, belly full, brain whizzing, heart bursting. I reckon I made it and I haven't even set foot on the court yet. Maybe that's what Aunty Milly meant when she said goodbye. When she said about every time she looks up into the sky she'd be watching for me. Maybe she meant those stars, they remind her of me. Maybe I'm gonna be a star!

I'm looking around the walls of books, watching

shadows, hearing street sounds I never heard before. Big mobs of people charged up . . . bottles breaking on hard corners . . . noise bouncing off brick walls. Cars honk different down here, more of that anger in them. Tyres make a tighter screech on cold bitumen.

That legend feeling's starting to slip right through me. I'm getting that heavy feeling in its place. That I'm-a-long-way-from-home, lost-in-the-big-city feeling in m'belly. I'm missing sounds I'm used to. Like . . . small mobs of people charged up . . . bottles breaking on tree trunks or hard heads, tyres skidding on dirt . . . I'm joking m'way out of that sad feeling that wants to settle down on me in the night.

M'mind's going crazy, but, crammed in here with all these other people's thoughts. I'm wondering what Aunty Em's brain must be like if she's got all these books running round her head.

I don't reckon I sleep all night. Somehow it's morning, but. I wander out. The place's quiet as. No one in sight.

There's a note on the table, that teacher-writing all neat and numbered.

1. I'll be back by four.
2. Help yourself to anything you can find to eat.
3. Here's the key to the front door. Make sure you lock it if you go out.

4. Garth won't be back till late.
5. Don't lock yourself out. If you go out take the key. If the door slams shut, it locks.
6. Rhonda is the name of the woman in the flat downstairs. She's very friendly if you need help. My number at school is . . .
7. Love you. See you soon. Aunty Emma.

I'm wandering around the flat checking everything out, wondering what to eat, where to settle. Too many choices. Aunty's got me worried about that key now. I'm not wanting to go out the front door in case something stuffs up and I can't get back in. We always got the windows open at home for climbing in. I'm not used to carrying keys.

I switch the telly on and watch a soap. Same soap as up home. Makes me feel like I haven't gone nowhere. I switch the TV off. I'm starting to wish Uncle had woken me up and taken me with him to the school he's performing at.

I'm thinking about writing a letter home. Telling them about the bus and the nun and Uncle's Merc and . . . I get excited and rush around finding some pen and paper from Aunty's study. I'm not calling it my bedroom yet.

When I sit down and face that big blank sheet of paper, I'm not knowing where to start. I'm not sure what it is that I've been doing. I'm not sure what it is about how

I got here that's worth telling. Seems too early to say how I am. I got no junga, no money to send them up, yet. I hold off on the idea of a letter.

I fold that blank sheet of paper and put it back in the study under my pillow. Won't be long, I tell myself, I'll have a page crammed full of what I'm up to and that envelope bulging with junga for them fullas.

I wander out the back steps. That sun's a lot softer down here, slanted off to one side. Makes it hard to know what part of the day you're up to.

I'm sitting down with another bowl of cereal. The woman downstairs's pegging out her undies on the clothes-line. I don't reckon she can see me pervin' from the top of the stairs. Then she looks up. I'm gone all shame, trying to look like I'm not watching. There's something about her undies I can't help spying on, but. A black lacy pair, and a g-string.

I'm hoping she's not thinking I'm doing

a job on Aunty and Uncle's flat. I try and say something friendly. Nothing comes out but a silly little squeak. She's giving me a smile now. Big wide smile, soft and open, and I'm realising I'm still thinking about that g-string and how it might look on her and now I'm all shame and choking on my cornflakes.

'Hello,' her voice is slow, wafting up the back steps like the smell of something yummy cooking. 'You must be the nephew?'

I'm nodding like a fool.

'Hello, nephew. I'm Rhonda.'

Lemon meringue pie. That's what her voice reminds me of. That sweet tangy smell that teases you all afternoon while it's cooking, stringing you along till it's ready to be eaten.

There's a lot of things I know I could be saying, like my name and where I come from and asking her about her day. But I can't find those words nowhere. They're all gone hiding, leaving me sitting out here like a munyard, getting my eyes caught up on her knickers.

☼

Next day, I hear Uncle rushing out the door.

'One day soon you gotta come out to school with me. Give me a hand dancing.'

I'm ready to race after him. The door slams. Too late.

One day soon could be a long way off.

Same time, I'm kicking m'self. I could've learnt a heap of deadly dances up at Yarrie. Always seemed like next trip I'd learn more. Always next time. Now I'm down here I'm cursing I didn't hang round those old fullas some more. Learn those dances that go way back.

I don't want to let m'uncle down. I don't know how I'd feel out in front of a whole class of kids, but. I'm still a kid m'self. They'd laugh at me. Specially if I have to paint-up with nothing on but m'little judda-jah, my jocks.

☼

I'm not feeling too deadly 'cause I don't look too deadly. I got none of the right gear. But I reckon, even if I looked too deadly, I wouldn't feel too deadly, 'cause I'm as scared as. It's my first day down the courts.

Uncle and me, we walk in the gym. That male sweat sucks the breath out of you. There're blokes down here have to duck their head when they walk under the ring, they're that big. Being frightened makes you shrink. I reckon I shrunk real bad.

Uncle's stretching. I never stretched in my life. Only thing I ever stretched was the truth when I got in trouble.

'You can get your black butt down here and stretch. Don't wanna see you pulling any hammies or putting your back out 'cause you're not warmed up.'

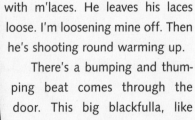

I'm following everything m'uncle does. He changes his shoes. He puts his painted-up runners on. The ones his 'cus, my Aunty Lillian, drew all our Story animals on in blackfulla colours. My real deadly shoes are still back there, in my Dreamtime. I got no shoes to change into so I fiddle with m'laces. He leaves his laces loose. I'm loosening mine off. Then he's shooting round warming up.

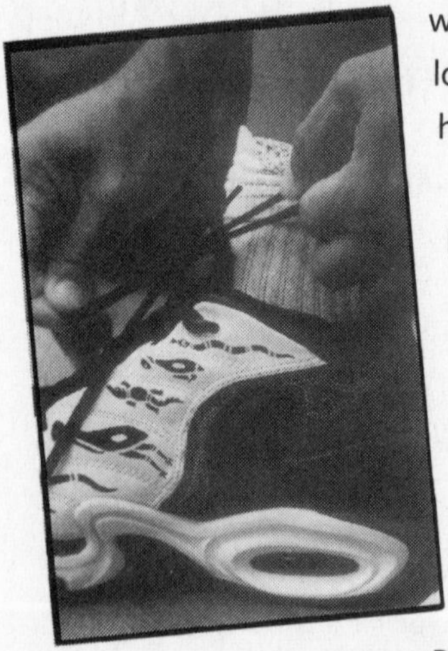

There's a bumping and thumping beat comes through the door. This big blackfulla, like American dude, Uncle calls him Leaping Leroy, walks in with a sound machine makes mine look like a toy. He's a mobile radio station. Looks like he's about to take off and drag us all to Mars. Bandanna, gold teeth, earrings . . . I never seen no one like this, not even in the movies.

He grabs my uncle, hugs him hard, thumping his fist into his chest right over his heart, 'Love, brother, love. Give me some love.' My uncle's buried under a mountain of all American black love.

Then Leaping Leroy comes up to shake my hand. I'm not sure whether I should run for it. He's got hold of me, but. M'hand's disappearing up his arm, he's pulling me in tight. He gives me a bro' handshake goes on for that long, twisting and turning, that m'arm takes a couple of minutes to find its way back to m'body.

Now he's slapping some other brother just arrived, laughing, talking trash, 'nigger' this and 'nigger' that. I'm looking round for who's hearing this. I only heard that word from the bulleymen or from people all puffed up and angry and wanting to hurt you. This big fulla Leroy, he's not hurting no one. He's in love with himself and the whole world. He's turning that 'nigger' word right round and sitting it on its head. Nothing can bring Leaping Leroy down.

'L-O-V-E, love. Love will heal the world, brother. Give us some love, man. Give it to me.'

I'm giving all I got.

Uncle introduces me to the whole mob of them. They all got time to shake my hand and slap me good. I feel like the new recruit.

I never seen anyone as big as Richie Rich. He wears that many rings and chains it's like he *is* the jewellery shop. The ball game's half over before he can get all that gold off of him to walk on the court. Tell him anything and he says, 'It's all good.' True. I reckon if you told him you slammed into a truck, broke both legs, and you only got a

day to live, that's what he'd say. 'It's all good, man.'

Uncle points out some of the others. There's Dray and the Landlord. 'In the key, under the net there, is the Landlord's apartment block. Anything that comes in the key, he throws out. The Boss, he looks like Bruce Springstein. Bobby Oh . . . whenever Bobby gets the ball everyone goes "ooohh!" Once he gets the ball he can take you in a heartbeat,' Uncle reckons.

'That fulla there, he's the Sultan of Swat. He can jump. That ball comes anywhere near the rim he swats it, sends it to the rafters.

'Only quiet one down here is the Guru. Used to be a monk. That's a monk not a punk,' m'uncle jokes.

I'm looking at the Guru. He's only a short fulla, not much taller than me. He don't look like no legend basketballer. Uncle reckons he's a point-guard. 'He doesn't say that much. When he says, you listen. The brothers call him the truth-speaker, see.'

I'm thinking that must be some special move I'm not knowing about yet.

After shooting around and warming up, Uncle tightens his laces. I tighten what's left of mine. Everyone's ready to play. Me too. I'm ready to run on.

Uncle cuts me off. 'You got some work to do on your own, boy. Wait here a minute till the teams are picked.'

Everyone else starts shooting from outside the three-point line. There a bit of trash-talking in the air, trying to make people miss their shots. The first five fullas to score a basket make up the first team, next five fullas to shoot play in the second team, see.

'Yo, yo, man . . .'

'No, no, man . . . no.'

'Give me the rock, man.'

'Yo, yo . . .'

I feel like a yo-yo in no-no-man's land! I'm thinking 'yo' must be somewhere between 'yes' and 'no'.

Those fullas who miss gotta sit down till the next game. No one's wanting to sit out. Rules of the game are first team to score ten baskets wins. Team to win stays on. Losing team swaps with the fullas waiting.

Uncle sends me over to the spare court. I'm dragging m'feet. He gives me a list of work-outs as long as m'arm, what I've got left of it. First some sprints up and down the court touching the baseline then the free-throw line – he calls them suicides. Then some shooting drills – left hand, right hand. Fifty jump shots from each of six positions around the key. Not in the paint, but. That's under the hoop, the keyway that's painted in on the floor in the shape of a key. Reckons I'm too small to be in there, in the paint. I'd take a pounding off the big fullas if I go in there. Dribbling drills, left hand, right hand. And if I got time, hook up with some other fullas hanging loose. Shoot round, play some one-on-one . . .

'Sharpen up your strengths, but work on your weaknesses, right?'

I'm trying to look eager as. But I'm wanting to be in the game, not dribbling on the spare court. This looks more like homework than basketball. M'uncle sees my hang-dog look.

'Remember, "Carry water, chop wood". Do what you gotta do. Work on yourself. That's what Phil Jackson, one of the greatest coaches in American basketball history, would say. That got him six championship rings with the Bulls and now two at the Lakers. Remember that.'

I'm flat out remembering m'name I'm that stuffed. I thought basketball was meant to be fun. I take a break, panting and sweating, sitting down watching m'uncle play with the brothers.

'You're a punk, man.'

'You're a P-A-M.'

'I'll tell you who's the punk arse mother . . .'

'That was *out*, man.'

'Kiss my black ass that was out.'

See, everyone's an umpire when you play pick-up. Leaping Leroy's going off over Richie Rich's call. I thought this was a game of L-O-V-E. Now Leroy sounds like he's about to kick everybody's butt over a leather ball filled with air going out of bounds. And I thought us blackfullas were crazy!

'It was *in*, bitch! I'm not kissing your black ass, nigger.'

Another nigg . . . I mean blackfulla said that, so that's okay, I think. I'm trying to find my way with this trash-talk.

Bald fulla, Ed-man, fires a dagger from way out, hits the rim hard, and shoots through the net like a knife. Next play he's got the rock, the basketball, slices through the key and jams one. He's shaking and baking, getting down and going crazy.

'This is too easy, man. It's too easy for me, man.' He's calling out at the top of his voice. 'Give me something I can play against. You better show me some respect today, man, 'cause I'm hot. I'm wiping the floor with you mothers, man. Someone should pay me for this!'

The others are revving him up, yo-manning, you're-the-man talk.

'I gotta sit my black ass down.' Ed walks off the court. 'Give the kid a go. This is too goddamn easy.'

I'm ready to take off on that plane, that big jumbo jet direct to Los Angeles, United States of America. The L.A. Lakers, I'm there. The crowd's crying out for me. I'm the man.

M'uncle steps in. 'Next time.'

The Guru walks over. 'Sometimes love, it's tough, man.' His voice is quiet. He sits down next to me. Un-laces his runners. I'm not sure if he's talking to me or to fresh air. The Guru, he has that way of talking he don't seem to worry if you're listening or getting it, he just keeps it flowing, slow and constant.

'You gotta put something in before you get something out, right?' He's towelling himself down. 'It's a hard school, this game of basketball. This game of life. You get it?'

I'm not sure what I get.

He keeps on gathering up his things, talking. 'It's a test, right?'

I worked out by now, he don't need me to answer.

'You gotta get the right mind-set before you can play the game. You gotta be a team-man.'

He gets up.

I'm waiting for more.

The Guru-man walks off.

I'm trying to figure something out from what I've been hearing. I never been thinking about that point-guard position. Me, I got m'mind set on flying through the air, through traffic, and throwing down some tomohawk dunks.

4

I couldn't get out of it. Aunty Em's got me on this train and we're off to her school. She reckons it might be a bit strange at first not knowing anyone there but I'm sure to make friends. It's not friends I'm worried about. It's what happens in the gaps between being with your friends, like when you're in class, from one bell to the next, sitting there being told you're stupid for hours on end.

We walk through the main gate. I let Aunty Em get a bit ahead. I've never been this side of the law before, arriving at school with a teacher. If she wasn't m'aunty, I'd be giving her a hard time. She's m'aunty, but, so I'm not sure what kind of time to give her. People are running up, the sucks, calling her Miss, asking her questions. She's got that teacher-face on now. She gotta look like she's in control or a real proper person.

I'm waiting, looking round, feeling like a dork. I never seen so much asphalt in my entire life. Wall to wall. And bricks. Not a blade of grass in sight. I'm wondering who's gonna be the first to pick a fight with me. Somehow I gotta keep my head from hitting that hard bitumen when they do. Wish Cedric was here. Least I'd have someone as my backstop.

Now I'm looking closer. These fullas're from everywhere. Blackfullas, whitefullas, brownfullas, yellowfullas, kind-of-orange-fullas, and every-other-colour-fulla in between, like fully. I wouldn't know where half of them come from. How did they get here? Why did they come? Where're they waiting to go to? Maybe I seen one or two look like Murri-fullas, I don't know, but.

Aunty Em turns, like she's been listening to my thoughts.

'Some Koori-fullas in your class. I'll introduce you.'

I'm glad I can hear that Aunty Em voice coming through, not that teacher-voice she's got for those other kids.

'Come with me first. We'll get the official business out of the way.'

I'm shaking in my boots walking up to the office. Here we go, I'm thinking. We head on in. Then I'm looking at that sign up above the front desk. I can read 'Welcome', that's it, but. I'm trying to get my head around all these other languages written up there. What is this place? The United Nations?

I'm starting to get it. Aunty Em teaches English as a second language. That's 'cause no one talks the same first language. Now I'm wishing I had my language. Mine got taken away, but. Aunty Milly told me stories of how our old people got punished for speaking their language. That was in the concentration camps, the reserves they hunted us mob into when them migaloos wanted our land. If the old people did their dances, sung their songs, spoke their language, they were locked up, heads shaved, punished real bad.

Down here, but, you can hear these kids talking their different ways all over the place. Even the asphalt looks like it's got its own language. Makes me sad as. Gives me that death feeling like I got nothing of me left.

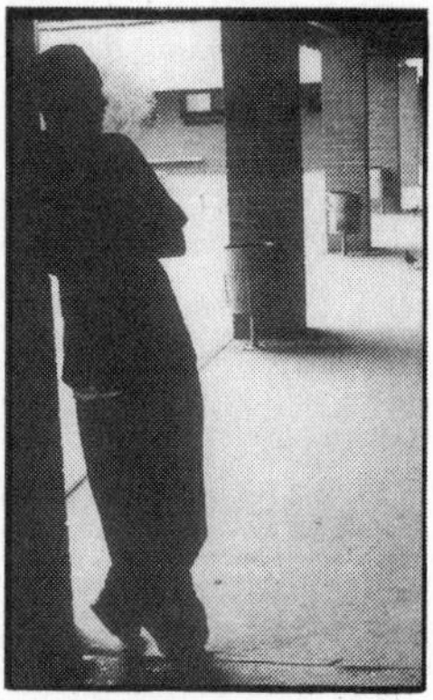

This tall fulla comes bowling out of the office. I step aside, but he follows, looking at me, with his hand out, grinning up big. He's got this hair chasing itself all over his forehead, bright ginger.

'G'day.'

Something about him makes me laugh. Next thing I'm sitting down in his office. I make sure Aunty Em's sitting right there beside me. He looks friendly, but you gotta watch your arse. I chuckle remembering stale-after-shave-and-hamburger-breath on the bus. And I'm chuckling 'cause I wasn't expecting to land in the Principal's office right from day one. Not to be sat down and told I was welcome. Also I'm chuckling 'cause I'm all over the place with knowing where I really am.

Soon as we get home, I grab Uncle's basketball and head down to that concrete slab of court along the foreshore there in the Pavilion. I gotta get off by m'self. I gotta think through the day.

I go through my work-outs to the sound of the sea, the salt taste on m'lips, the seagulls squawking overhead. I'm blocking out everything else. Just listening to the rhythm of the sea. Even a city as big as Sydney can't block that out. The rhythm of the sea, the bounce of the ball, the salt, the seagulls . . .

I am whoever I wanna be, I'm telling m'self. I can be that tall I gotta duck when I walk under that net. I can be see-through like the wind. I can be the ball, or the endless ocean, or I can fly overhead and crap on everyone.

I go to shoot a basket. There's no ring. It's gone. Someone's taken the ring away. That ring not being there, somehow that brings me crashing back down, two feet on the ground. Who am I kidding, I can be anything, anyone, anytime? As if! I'm a blackfulla. I can only be what other people expect me to be. And that's nothing too great. I can't even shoot for a hoop without someone shifting where the ring is. I'm getting m'self gooli-up.

Then I see her out the corner of my eye. The woman next door. The one with the knickers. Oh my-god, I'm thinking about her knickers again. I try to pretend I don't see her. Like I'm doing up m'laces and that. I sneak a look again. She's still watching, but, smiling at me. Standing there with a load of shopping in two string bags, one hanging off each shoulder, her in the middle. Out here in the open, she looks littler than I remember her back at the flats. Sort of little and alone in a real big place.

I'm waving before I want to, smiling up like I'm just a kid, forgetting I got m'self in that loser mood.

'No net?' Her slow voice drifts across on the sea breeze.

'Nup.' I'm not wanting to look dumb, like some idiot shooting around with no ring. Eh, good-go!

'They take it into the office. You just go to the front desk and ask for it. Leave a deposit.'

I'm thinking, *seagull deposit!*

I'm bouncing the ball, dribbling. Not that way! Figure eights between m'legs. Good-go! Imagining having the guts to front up to the person in charge and ask for their ring!

'If they leave the rings out,' she puts her load of shopping down, 'vandals break them off at night.'

She's settling in for a chat.

City's funny like that, eh? I never thought no one would bust-up on a basketball hoop. I busted-up on lots of things m'self. That basketball's sacred, but. That's meant to be for all us kids with bad attitudes. City fulla's got some funny ways.

I'm checking she's watching m'moves. Part of me wants to show off. Part of me wants to make sure I don't make a fool of m'self. Part of me wants to make her feel like I'm her friend and she's the same for me. Part of me tells me I'm a munyard for wanting to do anything.

'You walking home?'

She stops me in my tracks. I just stand here, holding the rock between m'hands, staring back, thinking walking home is not what I thought I was doing.

'Yeah.'

Why did I say that?

☼

Saturday morning, we got no milk. I go back to bed and think about things.

The whole block of flats was partying till late. Loud music. In and out of each other's flats. Strangers wandering through.

Rhonda, I remember her name now, well, Rhonda the woman in the flat downstairs, she showed me her place. Says she's a student or something. Not at school or nothing.

She's too old for school. Talked this science to me. About the planets and the universe and black holes and plants and how we breathe in what they breathe out and they breathe in what we breathe . . .

We sat on her couch for hours. I was into it, 'specially that stuff about the sky. Aunty Milly could've been talking about that. She might be looking up, seeing me as a planet like Venus with a halo of gases, or big Pluto right out there on the edge, or she could be seeing me as a black hole! Eh, good-go! That's rude!

Rhonda showed me photos of the pets she's had. Three-legged dogs, birds with no feathers, cats with no tail . . . She even makes friends with rats and cockroaches.

'If you're serious about protecting life, then rats and mice and cockroaches are part of the cycle of all living things. If you kill them then you can't call yourself a pacifist.'

I'm wondering if pacifist was something to do with the Pacific Ocean or whales.

'Or an environmentalist,' says Rhonda.

I'm knowing that's a greenie. I follow what she's saying. I just never had my thoughts shifted around this way before. She's telling me that's the way traditional blackfullas think. I'm not knowing if she's meaning me or not. I'm agreeing with her theory, but somehow I don't get what she's talking about. My Aunty Milly, when she tells me stuff about the way the world is, I get it. Aunty, she don't have theories that much, but. She don't call us paci . . . whatevers or nothing. She just tells it like it's always been.

Last night, sitting on that jalbu's couch, nothing seemed to matter that much, but. Mostly, I was wanting to be close to her, this Rhonda. Close to that warm smell of lemon meringue. Sinking into that slow, soft voice of hers.

I'm lying flat on m'back waiting for the day to happen. Everyone's sleeping in. I can hear those city noises out on the street. Traffic screeching. People yelling. None of it for me.

I've not been catching m'thoughts wandering back home. They musta been, but, 'cause now I got this dead-weight feeling in m'belly. Hits you when you least expect it, that missing everyone, homesick feeling. I got it that bad I'm even missing myself.

Sometimes I get that slack feeling. I'm happy to lay back and do nothing, just chill. This feeling is an ache, but. Like a bellyful of longing for that place means home. For saltwater. For that feeling of home-dirt under your feet. For the smell of smoke when that fire lights up as the sun goes down. For that same old food tastes of home. For those faces that know who you are without you having to do or say nothing.

Aunty Em comes out. Walks past in a daze. Checks the fridge. Slams the door shut. Goes back to the bedroom. Aunty shocks me back to here, where I am. She got those no-clothes on. She not even covering up when she walks by. Maybe I'm not here. Maybe I'm missing home that bad I've gone see-through.

'Just give us ten more minutes.' I hear Uncle roll over in bed, moaning.

'Ten more minutes could mean half the day with you and bed. I'm starving,' Aunty's groaning.

My belly's roaming. I can't take it. I gotta do something. If I keep on laying here I'm gonna be gone, don't exist no more, sunk into the same pattern as the sofa-bed. City makes you feel like that. Like you're nothing. I gotta get myself moving, walk away from that sick feeling of being somewhere you can't see your own self.

I can't get myself moving, but. Next thing, I hear the rattling of keys, Uncle's feet on the floor. M'feet swing over the side of the sofa, m'body sits up, m'shorts pull on, and I'm there at the door, going somewhere, anywhere.

'Can I come?'

Uncle nods. He's not talking up that much. Still half asleep. It don't matter.

We jump in the powder-blue. That sound of engine settles my belly down. Wheels turn, pulling away from the curb, houses slide by, we're moving. I'm sitting in the front seat of a Mercedes Benz, like flash as, like rich-fulla's car. I could be someone important. I'm with m'uncle. I am important. We're only going around the corner for some milk. Who cares? Could've probably walked. You see me complaining? No way. Me, I'm wrapped to be cruising, like fully.

We pull in next to the corner shop. Heaps of people looking at us now. I offer to go in. Uncle says he will. I'm cool with that. Gives me more chance to gammin' being rich and famous. Shades on, laid back, feeling good, singing up. Na na na na na, like I knew that I would now.

Eh, look-out! Uncle's back. I sit up. He's got his arms full. Paper, milk, bread . . . He's fumbling with the door. It's jammin'. I try to push from the inside. Uncle's pulling hard with both hands. The door busts open. Well, she can't be perfect. She's a Murri-fulla's car, not a bloomin' miracle.

Uncle gets in. Slips me a whole heap of change to put in m'pocket. Turns the key. Engine purrs. Slides her into gear. Accelerates. We're cruisin' again. What could be better? Sun streaming down, heads turning, us grinning up stupid on the inside, chillin' on the outside . . .

We come to this stop sign. Uncle looks to his right. I look right. I'm about to look left. Uncle don't look left or right, but. He's frozen, staring straight ahead. Then I see it. Bulleymen car, black mariah.

'Uh oh.'

Uncle's stuck. He don't move. He's mumbling to himself, checking. 'Seat belt's on . . . not blowing no smoke . . . registered . . . got m'receipts to prove I didn't nick the car . . . definitely got m'licence . . . not bombed up . . .'

That bulleymen's car turns left at the corner and

cruises right up to us, slows down, stops, middle of the road. A flash of blue light, quick burst of the siren to get our attention. As if we weren't watching! Just 'cause we're both staring straight ahead don't mean we're not watching when a bulleyman pulls up right next to you.

Uncle's getting gooli-up now, cursing under his breath. 'What do these bastards want now? Two hundred years they've been getting stuck into us. Can't they just leave us blackfullas alone. Always pulling us over for something. Picking on us just 'cause we're black!'

One look at that bulleyman uniform and I break into a sweat. Across m'forehead, m'palms, down m'back. I thought it'd be different down here.

We're still staring straight ahead. That bulleyman's taking his time. He winds down his window, slow.

Uncle turns, faces up to him, smiles, real polite-face. No way I'm looking at no bulleyman in the face, but.

M'uncle leans out the window, 'Yes, officer. What can I do for you today, then?'

Good-go! M'uncle's sounding like a whitefulla now.

The officer leans out and points to the top of the car. Real polite, true.

'Ah, sir, you have a carton of milk on your roof.'

'Eh, look-out!' M'uncle's feeling round on top of the roof for the carton of milk.

I'm thinking, geez, can you get arrested for that down here? I thought them bulleymen were bad up home!

'. . . thanks . . . thanks, officer . . .' Uncle's stumbling up on his words, whispering under his breath, 'Shame job.'

He grabs the milk, throws it onto m'lap, waves to the bulleyman, stalls the car. We kangaroo hop through the intersection, splutter up the road, not game to laugh at ourselves till we get home.

☼

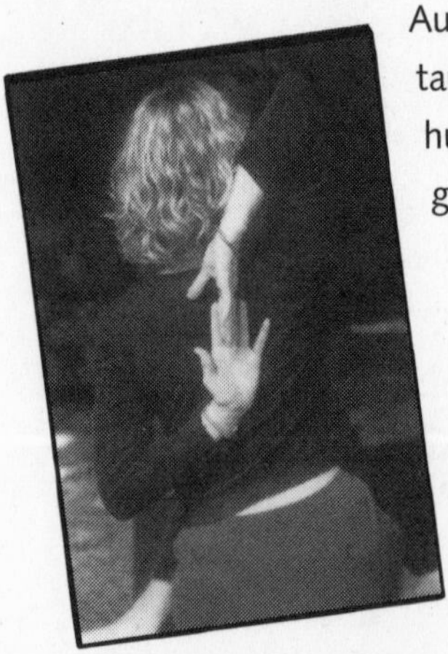

Aunty Em's down on the floor all tangled up. I'm thinking maybe she hurt herself or lost something. I'm getting down to help her.

'You want to join in?'

I'm not getting what's she's asking. She's got her moyu stuck in the air and I'm thinking this is something I shouldn't be looking at. I'm feeling shame as. Maybe I'm watching some women's business stuff.

'Yoga?'

Uncle's laughing up, 'Go on, get down there, have a go.'

I'm thinking, *good-go!*

Uncle's putting the kettle on. 'It's good for you. Stretching. Good for basketball. Makes you flexible.'

'You show him how,' Aunty's calling out to Uncle, her head poking out between her legs. I'm not looking, but.

'I done mine,' Uncle's got this sly grin on his face, 'before any of you slack fullas got up!'

The kettle's boiling. We sit out the back in the sun. I reckon before we've even finished up our first cup of tea, that bulleyman story's gone halfway round the flats.

Saturdays everyone hangs out. Rhonda hears us shiakking. She's come out for a cuppa. I'm gone all shy.

Uncle Garth tells the one about cus', cousin Greggie boy. He's m'uncle. He came down south and played some real good football. He was earning stacks of money, like fully. Sent a packet up to Aunty, his mum. She had this old bomb, rickety as. Traditional blackfulla car with dints and rust, see. The kinda car you gotta have a big mob riding in case he stops, and you need that mob to push start 'im. That is, if there's no bulleymen around!

Everyone's listening up to Uncle Garth. Smoko and Maori Mick come in from next door. Uncle's building up that story good.

'So, Aunty goes and buys a brand new car. Real deadly one. Radio, no rust, four doors open, windscreen wipers work, you can even wind the window down, and back up. When you driving, feels like you're floating on a feather. You don't feel no bumps. Even big potholes, he just cruise over.

'But no-good, Aunty had to get rid of that car. Bulleymen keep pulling her up all the time. "Where did you get this car, madam?" Like she stole it or something.

'She ended up selling that new car, going back to the old one. We in the back feeling those bumps on the road again. She reckons, "Better to feel them bumps in the road instead of them bulleymen bumps in your head."'

We're all laughing up. Uncle's repeating the line about the bumps in the head. Those Maori-fullas on for a good story. Rest of the morning we just sit around, cups of tea, dunking biscuits, yarning up. Those stories make me feel like my insides are starting to thaw. I stretch out, find a patch of city sun to soak in.

Rhonda, she sits down next to me and rolls a smoke. She reckons she liked us yarning last night. She's not big on parties and it was good to have someone to sit down with.

I'm nodding. 'True?'

If I didn't know she's old enough to be my aunty, I'd be thinking she was making a line for me.

She's asking me how I'm finding the city.

'Feels like I'm still arriving.' I'm telling her about the basketball. Her eyes are sparkling, like she doesn't think I'm silly wanting to be a legend. And I'm telling her about school and not knowing no one and not wanting to go there. And she doesn't try to tell me it'll be good for me. So, I'm telling her some more.

'I'll take you down the market.'

'Yeah?'

I'm not sure what I'm saying yeah to. I'm not sure what market or where. I'm feeling like she's the closest thing I got to a friend, but.

'Let's go.'

'What, now?'

'Better go now or it'll be closed. Get your gear.'

Aunty Em gives me that teacher-look. Like 'don't go getting yourself into trouble'.

Uncle's telling more stories to the Maori mob.

Rhonda gets up, laughing at Aunty Em. 'Don't worry, I'll look after him.'

I'm hearing Aunty mutter something, not sure what. I'm getting ready, but. Standing up tall, trying to make out I know how to look after myself, thanks.

Uncle grabs me on the way out. Hands me some junga. I know he's looking out for me.

5

I've never seen a place like the markets. Mountains of fresh fruit, vegies, cheeses that stink like your dirty socks, chooks caged-in next door to undies and overcoats, wild birds crapping and flapping right beside those tight little organic apples. Never knew that word 'organic' means 'natural'. I was thinking it might be something rude. Good-go, organic just means no way it's been cheating. Not like those other kind of fruit and vegies, the cheating ones that use drugs, steroids and stuff, to pump themselves up bigger and shinier to suck you in. Rhonda reckons if they can test Olympic athletes for drugs, they should be out testing what the rest of us are eating on our apples that we don't even know about. I'm wondering how you swab an apple?

There's people yelling from all directions. I'm thinking I done something wrong, they're yelling that fierce. Slowly, I'm getting that's just the city way of selling. I'm looking at those mangoes. No way I'd be game to front up and buy one, but. Might get m'self busted up. We knock 'em off the trees up home, mangoes. Many as you can eat. Down here they're selling 'em for gold.

Rhonda, she cruises, calm, sort of glazed look on her

face like the rest of the sea of people getting yelled at. I'm following close. Too close sometimes. I'm bumping into her, the crowd squashing me up against her back. I'm real shame at first noticing how warm and smooth she feels under that thin patterned dress. And her butt all bouncy.

But then I'm pushed and shoved and having to watch out for my own butt, that excited I'm not knowing which way I'm headed. I got eyes going all over the place, checking out, wondering where I'm headed and which way is home.

Rhonda stops every time she comes across a cage. Might be kitten, might be baby chicks, might be those goldfish swimming about waving their fancy fins. If it's alive she's there kissing the glass, cooing at pigeons, sticking her finger through the wire cage to touch a ball of yellow chicken-fluff. I'm looking round, shame. She drags me over, wanting me to stick m'finger through the wire same as her. I'm checking no one's staring first. People are flowing on past, but, not noticing, a long river of them headed for some ocean must be somewhere up ahead.

Fulla behind the stall's lookin' like he's seen it all. Deep furrows carved in his face, eyes darting. He don't care how much Rhonda cooes and carries on, it's the colour of her money he's waiting for. Same time he's working the crowd, fishing for some other mugs to reel onto his bank of the river.

Now Rhonda's shouting at some fulla wants to buy a duck. He's picked out the one she's making friends with. He's asking the stall fulla that owns the duck how to wring its neck or if he's gotta use an axe. Rhonda can't take it. She's pushing in front of him, shoving her purse out, asking how much. She's pulling at me, the tears choking her up.

'Do something. We gotta stop him.'

Whadda you mean *we*, whitewoman, I'm thinking to myself, backing off.

'Tell him! It's our duck.' Rhonda's yelling, pushing me at the stall owner.

I'm standing there like a goose, fumbling with m'words, never havin' got into a punch-up over a duck before.

☼

We're sitting in the bus, big cardboard box on our knees, something feathery and funky, flapping and crapping around inside, poking its beak out the airholes.

'2 Quack. What about we call him 2 Quack?' Rhonda smiles at me.

You'd reckon we'd had a baby.

I'm not getting the connection. We got this pure white duck and she's wanting to name it after this black American rapper. Modern day Martin Luther King, that's what I heard fullas call that 2 Pac. Does his scrappin' through rappin', but, fighting for the rights of his people, black people. Trouble is, he got shot by another rapper.

I'm looking at her now, this little woman next to me, this Rhonda. Creamy white skin, straight mousy hair, freckles and blotches. She's cute. One time I'm looking at her like she's m'big sister, or aunty, or just a friend. Next minute I'm looking at her like she could be my jalbu, my chicky babe. Most times I'm looking at her and she's looking like the strangest migaloo jalbu, whitewoman, I ever seen. And I'm feeling real black and she's looking real white and that means we live on different planets. Other times, all that colour stuff don't matter. We have that same way of thinking and feeling no matter if we're black or blue or green.

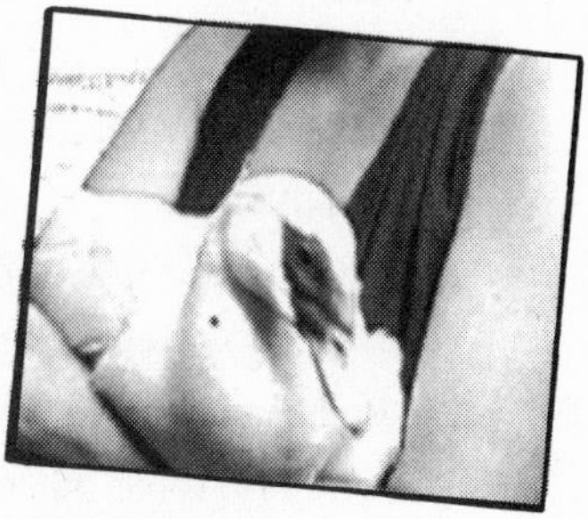

I'm babysitting 2 Quack. Over at Rhonda's. Rhonda's gone out to work. She works down the pub four nights a week, Wednesday to Saturday. She's not wanting to be a barmaid the rest of her life. It gets her by for now, but. I reckon one time I should go down there with her. When 2 Quack's settled in enough to be left on his own. I could sit down one end of the bar. I reckon I look eighteen. No law against drinking soft drink. I'd be with an adult. Rhonda's an adult.

Rhonda reckons it's not a great idea. She doesn't want to be leading me astray, setting a bad example or something.

Most days I'm downstairs at Rhonda's. Not doing anything special. Hanging out, playing with 2 Quack, just chillin'.

She's teaching me lots about the Internet. We play computer games. She's got heaps. Or go for walks around the cliffs. She knows all about algae and seaweed. She reckons seaweed is where it all begins. Like, you got no seaweed, you got no life. True, that's what she reckons. I never looked at it like that. We used to muck round up home dressin' up as girls with seaweed hair, teasing, chasing each other down the beach. Never saw that long slimy stuff like it's the source of all that's living and breathing. That's deadly.

We go wandering, shoot some hoops down the Pavilion. Rhonda knows the woman at the office. She gets the ring out for us. Don't even have to leave no deposit!

Rhonda knows a whole lot of people round here. We go to this cafe. You'd reckon it was her place. Some bloke, migaloo, with long dreads is sitting on a stool reading the newspaper. She pinches him on the butt. No-good, he don't seem to budge. Keeps on reading. 'G'day, Rhonda darls.'

Bloke that runs the place even knows what she wants to drink. I'm still getting m'mind around what's on the list.

I don't see no drink I even heard of before. I'm about to ask for a Coke.

'You want a coffee?'

I nod. 'Yeah.'

'Which one? Cappuccino, macchiato, moccha?'

I'm looking blank, making out I'm caught up with the cakes. Rhonda winks at the bloke behind the counter. Thinks I don't see her. Now I'm feeling like a real munyard kid.

'You want something to eat?' she's asking.

I got nothing to lose. 'Maybe a piece of that lemon meringue pie?'

I'm laughing up stupid with m'own private joke. I don't reckon she can read minds, Rhonda. She's not like that. Still, she's smirking at me funny.

She chooses a table outside and we sit down. I never sat in a place like this before. Must be where rich people come.

I'm sticking out like a goose. I put on the sunnies I borrowed from m'uncle. They either make me or break me. Make me look super-cool or a complete dork. I can't tell.

The bloke behind the counter calls out, 'Rhonda. Your short black.'

Eh, look-out! Who's he calling short!

'And your flat white.'

Eh, good-go! Now he's picking on Rhonda. I'm ready to G-O, take him on outside. Maybe I'm short. I can go, but. I'll knock him flat. Eh, flat. Did you get it? I'm deadly and I don't even have to try.

I'm checking out Rhonda. Is she gonna take him on or me?

She's laughing. 'Coffee? I ordered you a flat white coffee. Do you have sugar?'

Shame job! I try one of Cedric's old lines to chill m'way out of this hole. 'Yeah, sugar thanks. Honey.'

She giggles. 'That's sweet!'

Least m'jokes are working.

I offer her a bit of my lemon meringue.

She shakes her head. 'On a diet.'

'Go on, have a bit,' I reckon.

She takes her time, like a mouse, nibbling it off the end of m'spoon, looking up at me with those eyes.

Now we're watching people walk past. Somehow we got all embarrassed watching each other.

I'm not sure that I'm wanting to go. M'uncle's friend Kenny came round. He's a DJ. Got his own mobile unit. Does clubs, pubs, and every so often does a free gig down the Aboriginal hostel so the kids can raise money for pool tables and stuff.

Kenny's saying I should come down. They're having a disco this Friday night. Aunty Em's real keen for me to go. Same with Uncle. They reckon I could meet a few kids my own age. I'm not so worried about meeting kids. I'm happy enough just hanging around Rhonda and 2 Quack.

But I'm going 'cause I sort of owe it to them.

I dug m'heels in about school, see. One week was enough for me. Aunty Em tried her hardest to make me feel good and pal me up with fullas. I can't explain it that good, what I feel. Like I'm still travelling, not arrived nowhere. I've only just left up home, see. All m'mates. M'family. Half of me is back there in those broken up pieces. I'm not that ready to be getting m'self together somewhere new. I don't feel that right in myself so how can I be feeling right about facing the whole United Nations every day.

I can't see the point of school, neither. Rhonda's teaching me more than I ever learnt in a classroom, like fully. And it's more fun.

I'm thinking about asking Rhonda to come down the hostel with me to the disco. Nah! I'm changing my mind. Someone might think I'm walking in with an aunty. The disco's for under eighteens. I'd be too shame explaining who she is. 'Friend' is gammin', don't seem to say it like it is. She probably couldn't get a night off work, neither.

☼

Here I am, sitting off to one side, music blasting, hall filling up with dudes, and me on my own. M'flash, blue Wolverine shirt washed and ironed. Aunty Em did that for me. M'hair gelled. She gave me some of Uncle Garth's, plus a squirt of his after-shave. I'm looking and smelling that deadly I'm falling in love with m'self.

Strange, but. I was expecting to know someone. Like I know Kenny, 'course. He's busy up the front working the music, but. I'm interested in his gear. He's got some big amps. When I get my bearings I'll make my way over.

I was expecting to hear voices call out when I came in through the door, but. Up home I walk in somewhere, the whole place is calling out 'hello cus" . . . 'wichay, deadly budd' . . . yakaiing and all that. Here . . . nothing. Black faces everywhere but no one that knows me. Here I am, in a hall full of blackfullas, and I'm still the odd one out. None of my mob round here.

I'm sitting back in this corner, hoping no one's picking

me for a dork, feeling sorry for m'self. These fullas are all up, cruisin', dancin', hangin' in bunches. As cool as, some of them, true. Be nice to get to know a couple so's I don't stick out so bad.

Some of the adults, the organisers, come over and say g'day. Tell me I'm real welcome here. Kenny takes a break and introduces me round to a few. I'm loosening up. The cool dudes are sizing me up, wary. Thinking I'm gonna be stealing their jalbus 'cause I'm a drop dead spunk! Not!! Only gammin'. I can pick up the vibe, but. I reckon, only chance of a chicky babe round here is b-y-o.

You gotta respect that place you're on 'cause it's not your place, I'm hearing that aunty-voice now. Even though Happy Valley was sad, it was my place. Down here in the city you gotta watch your arse, true, that stale-burger after-shave fulla's right.

I'm brave, but. I'm a warrior man. I psyche myself up and sidle over to this shy jalbu looks like she's on her own.

'Dancing?'

'Asking?'

'Askin'.'

'Dancin'.'

Deadly! I get a chance to show off my stuff on the dance floor. Lucky I got sisters. I been up there dancing with them since I could walk. She looks impressed enough.

We take a break. Grab a soft drink. I'm about to ask her name. Five or six of the cool dudes crowd around.

Maybe one of them's her brother, I don't know.

'Comin' outside?' A short little punk fronts me.

I'm not answering straight off, 'cause I'm not sure what he's asking. No-good, I'm thinking I wouldn't mind rollin' him for his shirt. Only gammin'. It's red and shiny, with yellow-and-black patterns. Deadly. Designer label I seen on the ads.

'We got some stuff.'

I'm still not answering. I'm looking around. Some part of me is hoping somehow I'm gonna see Cedric's big forehead come grinning through the door. Any of m'cousins'd do. Even a sister . . .

She comes up close, the shy jalbu I've been dancing with. Says we should go outside.

I'm there.

So are the six others.

They're talking tough about nicking stuff and going up the Cross and all the junk they've tried. I know showing-off when I see it. And I'm seeing it all right. Technicolour, wide screen, surround-sound style of showing-off.

I'm hanging back, trying to get a bit closer to the jalbu. A joint's passing round, njarndi. I made my decision about that stuff way back when I was eight. Drugs, alcohol, the lot. 'No way,' I said to myself, 'I'm not going there.' I seen everyone charged up, punching and fighting and dying like flies in a thunderstorm of fly-spray. That's not gonna be me. And I've stuck to it.

When that njarndi gets to my turn, all eyes zone in on me. I take my time. Then pass 'im on without a puff. I'm cool with that. Think what they like. I'm not joining in to do no one no favours. Stuff that. They can do what they want, smoke it, eat it, drink it, shoot it up . . . I'm sticking with me.

'You thinking you too good for us?'

It's the little punk with the flash clothes. The one I thought might be her brother.

'I do my thing. You do yours.' I'm straight out with it.

'Smart arse.'

I can move fast, but not up against six of them. I knew I could handle myself with the little punk. He keeps mouthing off, but, about me not being from round here – *der!* – and thinking I'm that deadly I'm as good as migaloo fullas or some crap.

I'm having to hear all this doing the best I can. I give a few of them something to wake up hurting about the next morning, but. I give out as good as I get. Sort of. They're not trying to do me that much damage. Just showing who's boss, and who's place I'm on. I'm not arguing, neither.

Last I seen of the girl, she's standing back giggling in a silly sort of way like she'd set me up and now she's having fun seeing me get my butt kicked.

☼

I'm limping home feeling real sorry for m'self. Busted lip. No air getting through m'nostrils. Ribs hurting. Grazed knee. I feel like I gone fifteen rounds with The Man.

Up home I get busted up by whitefullas for being black. Down here I get busted up by blackfullas 'cause they think I'm trying to be white. I'm wondering what the hell is me.

And my shirt's ripped. I could take the rest. Bruises heal. M'new Wolverine won't, but.

I walk through the busted-up part of the fence. We got something in common, me and that broken brick wall. Across the path, up the steps, past the bullet holes . . . Things could be worse, I'm telling m'self.

Uncle and Aunty are cuddled up on the couch watching a video. They don't notice for a bit. I'm not showing them nothing, neither. Too shame.

Aunty picks it first.

'What happened to your shirt?'

'Got caught on the fence.' As if!

Aunty starts checking me out. Turns the light on. Drags Uncle away from the movie. She starts to freak.

'You're bleeding!'

I'm not surprised.

Uncle stays cool, calming Aunty Em down. 'Looks like he did all right for himself.'

I'm feeling better already.

'Who got stuck into you?' Uncle asks.

I build it up a bit. 'First of all there was a couple of

them. I was drivin' 'em, fixing them up okay. Then a couple of others jumped in. I turned round and there's a dozen or more. I'm thinking, no-good, I'm gone.'

'I know where you're *gone*.' Uncle sees straight through me. 'In the head!'

'No, true god.'

Aunty's looking like she's in a casualty ward. 'Be serious.'

'Who was it? Whitefullas?' Uncle asks in that detective voice.

'Nah, down the hostel. Blackfullas.'

'That's okay then.' Uncle grins. 'So long as it wasn't a bunch of racist white bastards! You're just earning your stripes with the mob down here. Well, in your case, your bandages!'

Aunty's getting gooli-up at Uncle mucking around. I can tell he's wanting to get back to the video. I'm happy enough to settle down on the couch with them. Now I'm home I'm not hurting that much. Aunty's real upset, but. She's getting a bowl of warm salty water and cotton-balls for bathing the cut on m'face. She's got some tea-tree stuff good for healing things.

'The cops, I can understand,' she goes on, 'or some other thugs. But when your own mob gets stuck into you . . .'

Uncle mumbles something about different mobs.

'Still, that stinks.' Aunty won't be put off.

'Guess it's a black thing.' Uncle smirks, still watching the movie.

Aunty Emma, she's not ready for laughing up. Uncle, he takes a long breath in, presses the pause button on the video machine and starts. He's got that look, that face ready to tell one of his munyard jokes.

'It's only a bit of blood, Em. Nothing's broken. Like this old fulla. One time, see, this old fulla, he went in the courtroom all busted up. Blood all over the place.'

I'm remembering this one. I'm giggling up already.

'And the judge, he looked at him too. Real stunned. "My goodness, what happened to you?" in a real judge-voice.' Uncle's taking his time, making sure Aunty Em's listening. She's holding out, putting the dirty cotton-balls in the bin, rinsing the bowl.

'Listen now. That old fulla reckoned, "I bin have a fight with my missus."

'Judge says, "Looks like it was a good one. How did you get to look like that?"

'"She bin hit me in the head with the tomato."

'"With the what?" the judge says.

'Old fulla says, "Tomato."

'Judge says, "How can one tomato do that much damage?"

'Old fulla reckons, "She never bin take him out of the can!"'

Aunty can't help herself, she's laughing up good. Uncle's not finished, but.

'The judge smirks, coughing and spluttering, trying to

hold it together. "Well, well, now, how do you plead?"

'Old fulla looks up. "I bin bleed everywhere!"'

Aunty's gonna break a rib, she's laughing that bad.

I'm feeling that laughter rub into me, into my wounds like ointment for the healing. I heard this story lotsa times up home. Used to be one of Uncle Budda's favourites. Hearing m'Uncle Garth tell it now makes me feel like home's not that far away.

The three of us, we lay back on the couch, Uncle and Aunty cuddling, me nestled in, watching the rest of the movie.

6

Saturday and we're all hangin' loose, cups of tea, yackin'. Smoko and Maori Mick are over. Some other teachers . . .

Rhonda gets a shock when she drops in. Somehow seeing me busted-up brings those tears to her eyes.

Weekends, we don't get much time together, Rhonda and me. Aunty and Uncle are around. There's a feeling in the air, a kind of smell, or maybe more like something's spilt on the floor and everyone's watching their step, pretending not to notice. None of us've said nothing. Just is that Rhonda and I know weekends are more for me being round at Aunty and Uncle's. She and me, we back off each other come the weekends, see.

Rhonda's down the pub from Saturday afternoon till late. Before that, she's listening to the Science Show. Sundays is for her sleeping. I woke her up in the middle of the morning one time. She reckoned it was that early it must still be yesterday.

I'm thinking, I gotta be getting a game with Uncle and the brothers this time. I can jump higher than most of them fullas. I can handle the ball good. I'm quick at passing. What's the hold-up? All I do is these drills m'uncle gives me to get m'shooting touch.

He reckons I gotta get the ball spinning, rotating back. It's gotta be all net, never touch the ring. Fifty shots from one position then I can move onto the next. Good-go!

'Like our traditional stories, these work-outs,' he's telling me. 'You gotta listen over and over again. You gotta shoot the ball over and over again, then go to the next position.' I'm not getting it. Traditional Murri-fulla stories are like basketball?

He's watching me, too. He's got one eye on the game he's playing, one eye on this court over here, seeing if I'm giving it my best shot.

He's off for one game. Comes over, in m'ear. 'Imagine a wave starting at your heels. As you push up with your knees, the wave gets bigger. As your arm extends up into the air, the wave does too. When your body's all stretched out, the tip of the wave should be where your rude finger is.'

Good-go! I'm thinking. You know what you can do with that rude finger! Now he's got me out surfin'! I thought we was playing basketball or telling stories. Not out surfin' as well!

Uncle was stirring Aunty Em the other night. Telling her us Murri-fullas invented surfing.

Aunty goes, 'Yeah?'

Uncle goes, 'Yeah, true god. We been surfing on those turtle shells long before you fullas thought of surfboards. Like you fullas always do, you stole the good idea off us.'

Aunty believed him, too. Sort of.

☼

Come Monday, Rhonda and I get time to be back together. I still got the bandaid over m'cut and she's still into saving-me mode. I'm not minding, neither. I love her fussing.

'Why didn't you ask me to come with you?'

''Cause you were working.'

'You know I can swap with someone else when I want a night off.'

I'm making out there was no way I knew she could take time off. I change the subject. Tell her about the lemon meringue. Only that it's my favourite pudding, not that other stuff about me thinking she smells as good.

She makes me lie down on the couch. I'm feeling real slack, just laying back. Not that homesick slack. That good-to-be-here slack.

Rhonda goes off down the shops to get a video and some lemons. Reckons she'll cook me up a lemon meringue pie. *Aw, come-on!* I'm sounding like a real munyard in m'mind.

2 Quack's tucked up next to me. I never heard of anyone letting their duck come inside the house. And on their

couch. Rhonda's pretty fast on the pick-up. Soon as he goonas, she's there with the toilet paper picking it up. If it's just me and 2 Quack here, I'm looking the other way, gammin' I never seen nothing.

Sitting with this duck on m'lap, I'm thinking that smell of warm feathers is pretty good. I'm starting to see 2 Quack through new eyes. He's got into this pattern now. Gets up about the same time as Rhonda. Makes it outside by midday. Waddles back in when the sun's going down. Settles in for a night of TV on the couch.

Rhonda's got the coolest TV. It's a two-in-one. Two TVs, one on top of the other. The top one's got the best sound. Other one's got no sound, good picture but. I'm not watching that much. More dreaming about lemon meringue and how I'd be telling Cedric about Rhonda.

She comes back with a bag full of groceries. Tim Tams for us till the pie's cooked. Lebanese cucumbers for 2 Quack. I don't know how come she got to know that 2 Quack's into Lebanese cucumbers. Why Lebanese is better than just cucumbers, I don't know. Rhonda, she's good on picking treats, but.

I help grate and squeeze the lemons. I have to do them just right, the way Rhonda says. Not on the big holes of the grater, on the small spiky ones that leap out, grab bits of your skin and make a mess of mincemeat out of you. I take a turn at beating the egg whites till they go stiff. She mixes the butter and sugar, calling out like one of those surgeons on the telly for what she needs. I'm wondering how I'd look in a nurse's uniform. Good-go!

The pie's baking in the oven. Rhonda starts the video. We sit together on the couch. Not touching. Close, but. She says she's cold. I just sit there frozen, not knowing if I should try and warm her up. I got too many jokes running round in my mind to move. She waits for a bit, then gets her doona. Double-down, she reckons, the best. I'm not saying nothing, but I'm thinking that 'down' gotta mean 'duck', duck feathers. I could be wrong, but.

She gives me some doona.

I'm trying to keep my mind stuck on that movie. It keeps wandering down under the doona, but. She's snuggling up. The main characters in the movie are getting smoochy. I'm not knowing where to look. I'm getting as hot as. I'm gonna explode or burst into flames or somethin'.

She presses pause. Looks up at me. Like she's waiting for me to do something.

Then she announces, 'Pie's ready.' She climbs out from under the doona.

Thank god! I wasn't sure what she was gonna say. I'm getting up. I need to get some air.

'Stay there,' she slips out to the kitchen.

I can hardly breathe. I'm thinking, Run . . . Stay . . . Run . . . Stay. And then I'm thinking, *Stay*. Cedric'd give his bottom dollar to be in my shoes, or is that in my bare feet? I gotta be a man. It's not just my reputation on the line.

I gotta do it for my cus'. I'm giggling under my breath, lying out on top of the doona.

My mouth's watering with the smell of warm pie. Rhonda comes back from the kitchen, a big pile of lemon meringue on one plate. No-good, only one spoon, true. And a sweet smile across her face. She's wanting to feed me. I'm well able to feed myself, busted-up or not. She insists, but.

Rhonda's got double everything today. Double cream to go with the pie. We never had double nothing, not even half-cream, when m'mum made lemon meringue. I'm getting the feeling I'm double or nothing with this jalbu. Eh, good-go! Now my mind's going wongy.

'Yummy, eh?' Rhonda's licking her lips.

'Mmmm.' My mouth's bulging with hot meringue and cold cream.

I'm watching the spoon disappear into her open mouth, her soft lips closing round. I'm doing the same when it's my turn. Taking my time, thinking things I only dream about. I'm thinking she's thinking the same things. Somehow I'm not going all shame, but. Only when I think of Cedric watching.

From now on it's different. There's no way back to that boy I was. My mind's been switched on, all lights blaring.

Before it was a big dark hall, me moving around by touch, bumping into things. Now I've woken up and I'm somewhere I never been before. I'm a man. *The* man. I got a jalbu. And a duck. I got that much I'm looking at, I'm not sure what it is I'm seeing.

I'm trying to focus m'eyes onto just the three of us. Her and me and the duck. Not that we're planning anything, nowhere to go, or do, or nothing. We're just here, together. I can't take on much else. One day rolls into the next and that's enough.

I'm wanting her to play some more computer. I'm right into this skateboarding game. Gammin' skateboarding's gotta be better than busting your butt getting a nose grind happening. And me with no board! Here on the screen I've got my kick-flip McTwist down fully, good as.

Rhonda's rolling a joint. She's right into njarndi. I'm sticking to my beliefs, but. I don't do drugs. She don't tease me, or say I'm a wuss or nothing. Just puffs away herself. I'm noticing how bad it tastes when we kiss after she's been smoking. I'm wishing she didn't smoke. I'm buying her lots of peppermints to suck. She's getting the hint. Talking about giving up smoking and how good I am for her. Can you get with that? Good-go, I never thought I'd be good for no one. I'm thinking I should write home to Aunty Milly or to Mum or to someone. I reckon Rhonda's the best school report I ever got. They'd be real proud of me. I think.

Rhonda, she's sinking back into the couch, but. She's in that mood she wants to talk about herself. I'm trying to concentrate on saving my butt from the predator.

'I suppose you and I have got a lot in common,' she says, trying to drag me in.

'Aw, come-on!' I'm jivin' her, like she could be meaning something else we got in common, like under-that-doona feeling.

She don't laugh, but. She's got her mind on serious.

I got m'mind on the game.

She's gone all quiet.

I grab a quick look around, checking she's okay. I see this mob of tears backing up behind her big, blue eyes.

'We've got no one to love us. No one wants us, you and me, do they?'

I'm trying to nod yes. I'm thinking of m'mum and aunties and uncles and m'whole mob back home, but. I'm not wanting her to feel like she's the only one left out. So I make some noise, could be 'yeah' or 'uh ha', or 'mmmm'. Sort of leaving it open. Hoping like hell I can get on with the game.

Now she's stroking m'face. Saying how beautiful my hands are. And m'dark brown eyes. And I'm looking at her now, the tears rolling down her pink cheeks, and I can feel things stirring in me. There's no one around to tease. No big mob of sisters, no uncles, no aunties, no Cedric, not even in m'mind. No one but the image of me in her eyes.

And I'm living up to that image. I'm seeing m'self like I never seen m'self before. She's making me into that warrior man.

And she's crying, wanting me to hold her. And we're kissing and I'm getting good at it. And we're talking like we never talked before. About inside things. About her being lonely.

Rhonda, she don't have a family, she don't reckon. I'm thinking, how could that be?

'I've got a mum and dad, of course. Everyone has.' The tears keep rolling down her cheeks. I keep wiping them away. 'But somehow my life isn't turning out the way they wanted it to be. It worked out for my big sister. She's married with kids and a house and a car and all the things you're meant to have. Me? I got scared of that. I wanted to see if there was something else. It didn't work out that way for me.'

Rhonda, she reckons she's the black sheep of the family. I'm looking at her pale skin and eyes all pink with crying. *Black?* I'm thinking. *Good-go!* Maybe that's like calling a white duck after a black rapper. I'm starting to get that nothing's-what-it-looks-like feeling. 2 Quack could be the black duck of the family! *What have I got m'self into?* I'm thinking. I got a migaloo jalbu could be a black sheep and a white duck could be a black rapper. Me? I thought I was a blackfulla. Could be I'm an any-fulla or a no-fulla or a someone-else's fulla. I'm getting myself real jumbled up.

I'm mucking round in my mind, trying to get a hold on her way of thinking, but. There's no way I can imagine not having your mum and dad and sisters and brothers and all your cousins, the whole mob of them there to back you up. No family? I'd be dead, like fully.

Only time Rhonda sees her mob, she reckons they make her feel like a capital L loser. The way she dresses, what she thinks, the food she doesn't eat. She doesn't eat meat, see.

Rhonda's thinking she won't go back home for Christmas this year. Her home is the next big city south. Melbourne.

'What's the point? I don't eat turkey.'

I'd be crying if I wasn't laughing.

The corner of her mouth twists up in a sort of half-smile.

'You might laugh, but it's true. I'm the odd one out. That's what I mean. You and me are meant to be. We're both outcasts.'

I'm baulking at that. Outcast? I'm trying to think how that sits with those migaloo fullas always wanting to call you half-caste, quarter-caste . . . telling you how to measure what's in your blood. Maybe 'out-caste' is like worse. Next to no-caste. Gone see-through or something. My mind's getting stuck, twisting up with these Rhonda thoughts. She's too deep for me.

Now, she's hugging, but, and I'm trying to hold on.

And she's stroking, and I'm trying to make out what she could mean about us being the same. And we're kissing, and I'm giving in, sinking into a softer place where thoughts, they don't matter no more.

☼

I'm dead asleep. Swimming in warm lemon meringue pie. I'm sliding towards it, but. The dark jagged edges of m'dream.

I'm hearing that knocking, nagging at me. I'm pushing it away, thinking it's them big bulleymen fullas coming for me.

That knocking keeps on at me. I'm hanging onto that sweet smooth creamy part of the dream I never want to finish. It goes dark, but, the thumping's getting louder. That language voice of one of the old fullas from up home starts. I can't get what they're telling me. I'm trying to call out. There's the knocking. I've gone all dry in the throat.

Then I'm sitting straight up, looking around. I musta crashed at Rhonda's. There's no sign of her, but. Maybe she's gone to work.

There's the knocking at the door. I'm hearing Aunty Em's voice calling out. Something about dinner.

'Coming . . .' I'm groaning. I'm getting that Uncle-don't-wake-me-up sound in me.

I'm feeling for m'shorts and t-shirt. Pulling m'self up.

Looking around for what time it could be, night or day.

I open up the door. Aunty Em, she's still there, looking at me sort of tragic, worried. I'm not looking back, but, 'cause I'm not wanting to answer no questions.

I'm following her back up the stairs.

I've been avoiding m'uncle. That's not hard. He's busy as, off early in the mornings. He gets home after school and crashes out, sleeps for a couple of hours.

When Rhonda's home, I just hang out there. Come night time, she cooks something up and we muck around and before you know it the night's gone. Too late to wake Aunty and Uncle up rattling with the key at the front door in the early hours. I'm getting slack as, laying around at Rhonda's.

Aunty's cooked up a big dinner. Uncle and I tuck in. No one's talking that much. Uncle reckons he's really stuffed from a hard day's work. Aunty's chewing something over in her mind. Me, I'm waiting for the storm to break. For them to come crashing down on me with a big lecture.

I'm not telling Uncle I'm getting lazy with my work-outs, neither. I'm looking more for fooling around, but. If no one's down the Pavilion, I get Rhonda on the court, mucking round, one-on-one. Not serious. You can't be serious playing with Rhonda. I don't reckon she's ever shot a hoop in her life. It's fun bumping into each other, me going for the ball over her head.

I'm still waiting at the table. No-good, Aunty, she looks at Uncle, sour as. Then gets herself stuck into the washing up, bossing those dishes around like a mob of kids cutting up rough at school. Uncle, he just checks to see I got enough money and cruises back to bed.

Between Uncle and Rhonda, I'm as rich as I've ever been. It's not the money I'm wanting that much. It's to be like him. Cruising off somewhere important each day. But I'm not pestering Uncle to take me or nothing no more. I'm hanging with what I got. And what I got has both m'hands full, like fully.

7

Days turn round to nights and nights become our days. It's our day-time, like maybe night-time. We go hang out up at Smoko's flat. It's cool as, here. Couple of people on the floor playing the guitar. Couple of others just cruisin'. I'm checking one woman out. I swear she's singing that song same as that jalbu sings it on the radio.

'That's her. She's famous.' Rhonda tells me.

I'm wanting to hold tight round Rhonda. She's showing me people, taking me places I've never been.

Smoko and Maori Mick are cursing about the bastards ripping off the country, making the rich get richer and us fullas get poorer. I'm agreeing.

There's a bloke, Zed, laying back on the couch. Real cool dude with long black dreads all beaded up. He's chatting on to whoever's listening.

'Man, I'm that energised, I gotta watch myself,' he reckons. 'I don't want to blow it all at once. I haven't felt this energised in weeks. No use wasting it. I think I better just sit this one out here on the couch.'

Rhonda's laughing, whispering in m'ear. Reckons Zed's always out of it. I think I know what he's saying, but.

Sometimes it's just best to sit with what you got, and imagine the rest.

Zed and me, we get yarning. Rhonda wanders over to sing along with Reggie and them on the guitar. That fulla, he can play the guitar real deadly. He picks the spot that makes the sound just right.

'That's what I'm like on the basketball court,' I'm telling Zed. I'm not sure he's getting it. Don't matter. I keep on with m'talk, telling him I'm music to the ears when I got the ball.

'I'm the young gun.'

I check Zed out. He don't seem to be disbelieving nothing. He's just nodding, and yeah-man-ing, and gazing round the room.

I keep going. 'I'm the one with the hot hands. Microwave. That's what they call me. All you need to plug me in and turn me on is give me the ball.'

Zed's agreeing. Something about the waves down Bondi rolling in real big this morning. He's talking his talk. I'm talking mine. It don't matter that our talks don't match up I don't reckon. We're both on the same couch.

'When it comes down to money-time, with five seconds on the clock, I'm the money-man. Only I don't give no change!' Eh, look-out. I never knew I could talk up this big.

Now I'm jarring m'own self up. I'm talking that way, seems I already done it. It's fun talking like your dreams are what is, but. Fun as doing it. More, 'cause it's less hard work. I'm not needing to go down the Pavilion to practise. Seems I can practise with Zed right here on the couch.

Rhonda sends some fulla over to ask me to blow the didj, join in the jam session.

I'm telling him, 'Yo, I can blow. Just not right now.' *As if!* I'm forgetting I'm kidding m'self sometimes.

Misery must be being a Murri-fulla and not being able to play the didj. Maybe tomorrow I'll get myself learning off m'uncle.

I'm asking Mick about those Maori tatts across his face and what they mean. I'm wishing us Murri mob had something right out there in your face like those tattoos. Something you can see straightaway, says, 'I'm tough. Don't mess with me.'

'That's what I want.' Rhonda butts in, njarndied up. 'We could get something matching, don't you reckon?'

Something's holding me back. Maybe it's just I don't know what we'd get, what tattoo. I'm thinking I'd be wanting a frog.

I give her my girragundji test.

'You into frogs?' I'm asking.

See, I had a girlfriend when I was a kid. She dropped me 'cause she reckoned I got warts on my fingers from touching m'pet frog too much. I never forgot her dropping me 'cause of m'frog.

'Frogs?' Rhonda gets that shine in her eyes. 'Frogs are the most important creatures on earth. Do you know, frogs are the bio-indicators of the health of the whole world?'

She could've just said yes. That's all I was after. Rhonda gets hold of a frog theory from somewhere, but, and she's off and racing.

'They're disappearing. Have you seen any around lately?'

I'm starting to tell her about my girragundji, but there's no space so I stop. I'm not sure what she might do with the story of my pet frog neither. 'Specially if I tell her I still listen out for my girragundji's voice on the inside. And about the dreams I'm having each night, waking up, my mouth gone dry for words, not able to understand that inside voice no more.

'There's too much pollution in the world. If there's too much pollution for frogs, there's too much pollution for us. They're finding deformed frogs in the Amazon, mutations. An extra leg growing out of their stomach.'

Rhonda's looking up at me like I should do something about the pollution in the Amazon.

I'm looking back. All I can think of is mutant ninja frogs! I'm trying to joke m'way out. It's not working, but. Rhonda's looking serious. How do migaloos get their minds into thinking like this? This way of saving places they never been or seen or walked across or swum in?

I'm breaking into a sweat, thinking of my girragundji

mutating. I'm feeling like I'm growing legs where they shouldn't be. I'm in some computer game, or lost in someone else's jungle, or a legend up in big lights, can't find my way down off the billboard.

I'm getting myself real lost.

Rhonda's talking on about how you can't eat nothing without poisoning yourself and the world's stuffed.

I'm feeling that world she's talking about is inside me. I'm trying to focus on something. Something strong to hang onto. I'm focusing on tattoos. Just to keep m'mind together. A girragundji tattoo. A little green tree frog. No words, no telling what it means, just what it is. Green and slimy. A sign. Some way of people knowing I'm me, and I'm tough, they gotta watch out. I spent too long with my tattoos on the inside, I'm thinking. Maybe that's why I can't understand that voice inside me no more. I gotta get it out. Make a sign. Tattoo my frog to the outside, on my shoulder or over m'heart.

Rhonda decides on an Aboriginal flag tattoo. Black for the people, yellow for the sun, and red for the earth. She wants the yellow part of the flag shaped in a heart. My initial in the middle. Tattooed on her butt.

I'm getting scared.

Rhonda's coming close. Her arms round m'kneck. Dancing. Talking these poetry words. Reckons she's got this poem going round and round in her head all about me. Most of it I'm not following. Romantic stuff about my Dreamtime eyes. Something about me walking naked in a world that's done me wrong. Good-go!

I'm thinking, I can see m'self a bit like that, but. I'm into that feeling of being wronged. What's the world ever given me? A kick up the backside, that's all. Stuff trying to do something with my life.

I'm sinking into that feeling. That lost feeling. Looking for someone to save me. Real sorry for m'self. The last of us warriors. I'm picturing me dying, carried up high in a coffin, everyone crying. Me a legend. They'd have to take me back up home, bury me over with all those other fullas under that cement there. They could say some real deadly things about what I could have been.

We come back down to Rhonda's flat and crash. I'm fighting off that sleep, but. Not wanting to sink into that dark place. Dying is one thing. Getting caught up in your own bad dreams is something else.

Those dreams are taking me over. Every night now, the same. Starts all smooth, crystal clear sea, waves lapping, running, shiakking along the beach, with Cedric, or Rhonda, or my other bungies. Having fun. I'm hearing that girragundji voice and I'm strong and I feel good.

It never lasts, but. It always turns bad. The words go all wongy, the tape gets tangled up in the sound machine. And the dark comes down. Fullas that I can't see are chasing me. Grabbing me, hurting, rubbing m'face in something worse than dirt. Kicking me. I'm struggling to get out, to get away. I'm running. M'head pounding. I'm hearing that language, old fulla language, like some voice reaching out to me. It don't make no sense, but. I can't understand the words. I'm getting gooli-up. Like that voice's teasing me, disappearing back in time somewhere I can't follow. I've got none of m'own language. Not just that language from way back, from the old people. But the language of me now, from the inside. I'm trying to call out. I can't, but. I'm running too fast. I got no words to call with.

I'm punching up the pillow. Hitting out. Could be any time of night or day I wake up sweating and sobbing. My heart breaking.

I could be awake. Could be I'm sleeping, but. I'm near the front door. I've been hearing the knocking again. I'm gonna face up to them this time. I don't care how big they are. I'm gonna take them on, offer them out.

I swing the door open ready to G-O, fists up.

It's Aunty Em.

She jumps back. Me too, same. We frighten the living daylights outta each other.

I'm looking down, too. It's okay. I got m'boxer shorts on. For a minute there I'm thinking I could be naked.

'It's Friday.'

I'm blinking. Must be morning.

'You said you were going to come with me today.' Aunty Em's got that I'm-not-gonna-go-away look on her face.

'Where?'

I'm having a hard time trying to get a hold of where I am, let alone where I should be.

'Come on. You've got time for a shower and some breakfast if you want.'

I'm following Aunty Em up the stairs in a daze. Least I know I'm awake and not back there getting beat-up by m'pillow.

☼

I don't know how Aunty Em got me out on this platform waiting for her train. I swore, no way I'm going back to school. She reckons she said she'd pay me to come and talk to her class about culture, my Murri culture. She said I said yes. Must have been I got knocked out by the idea of some school paying me, the no-good Murri-kid with the bad attitude, to talk to a class.

That musta been what got me this far, waiting for some train, heading back to where I don't want to be. Back to school.

Aunty starts asking me things. I'm not knowing where to start with answers, but. Like what I'm planning to do? Do I want to get a job, any job, like in one of the local shops, maybe supermarket or the newsagents?

I'm not wanting to talk. I'm getting restless sitting on this bench. I've been sitting on too many benches.

I been feeling this habit coming on. This wanting to stand on the edge of things. Started there walking along the top of that sandstone wall around the beach. Daring myself. Walking out beyond the barriers. Balancing. Seeing if I lose it. Wanting to be caught.

I freak Rhonda out sometimes, standing on the edge of cliffs. She grabs me. Holds me back. I'm not seriously thinking of going nowhere. Just testing, her and me. Teasing. When she grabs me, we end up hugging, real tight, kissing and that. I watch the tears in her eyes. She reckons I'm the most important thing in her life.

'Even up there with 2 Quack?' I'm joking.

Aunty Em's still asking. I still not got no answers.

I wander along the platform. I gotta keep moving. I'm not wanting to talk about what I can't answer in my own mind.

I'm getting closer to the edge, standing with my back to that tunnel the train'll come out. Aunty Em's over there sitting on the seat. I can feel her getting edgy. I'm not thinking about puns or laughing or nothing, neither. Edgy? You get it? This time, I'm not joking myself out of m'mood, but.

My back's to the on-coming train. I'm right there where cement platform ends, drops into dark. I'm looking at that edge, that line where one thing becomes another. I'm balancing on that thin line, one foot on the ground, other foot lifted off. I nudge m'foot closer, some of it lapping over, feeling the weight of my body, that instinct hugging back towards the platform, the other part of me leaning out, daring.

If I look ahead, keeping my balance, I see a tunnel with no light at the end. If I look down, slowly, I see a gleaming ribbon of steel running across a jungle of dirt and grime. It's only a metre or more down. Falling wouldn't hurt nothing if there was no train coming.

Aunty Em's fidgeting, flicking her ticket. Other people are standing around, shuffling their feet, looking away or reading papers. Not seeing nothing they don't want to know about.

I'm hearing it in the distance. I'm keeping my balance, but. It's coming full pelt.

I'm wondering how I got to be the one out here, hanging off the edge? I'm wanting to be back over there with the rest, with Aunty Em. Doesn't she know, she's the only one. She's my only way back? I'm counting on her. She's gotta say something, do something, be the one to tell me I'm an idiot. Come and grab me.

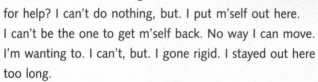

I'm hearing the rush, the pounding on the tracks, the monster thundering closer. She's gotta grab me quick. Don't she know I'm asking for help? I can't do nothing, but. I put m'self out here. I can't be the one to get m'self back. No way I can move. I'm wanting to. I can't, but. I gone rigid. I stayed out here too long.

I'm hearing it loud, deafening. I look up at her, pleading.

'Stop it!' she screams, the whole of her, and she's right

there, grabbing me back. I'm falling on concrete. On the safe hard cold living side of cement. Not that buried-dead side.

The train hisses to a stop.

Aunty's dragging at me. I'm getting up. Dazed. I didn't think she'd make it over to me in time. I'm looking at her red-hot face, alive and steaming.

'Come on.' She's hissing through tears and clenched teeth, air puffing out of her like that train with its brakes on.

I'm not blaming her. She grabbed me. She can yell and scream and say what she likes. Give me a good hiding. She's my aunty and she saved me.

She's not screaming, but. Just pulling me up and getting us outta there. Away from all the mob staring but not looking. Aunty's shaking. I'm more watching her than me. Looking for how it might feel to have those tears come bursting out of you. 'Cause I'm not feeling nothing. I'm thinking I might have died already, on the inside.

She's not knowing what to say. I'm not knowing, neither. I couldn't be the one to pull me back, that's all. There's gotta be someone that can save me. I don't know how to say that to her. I'm hardly knowing how to say it to m'self.

Back home she cools off. Phones the school. Cancels coming in. Now I'm feeling like a weight around her neck.

The cuppa tea's good, but. Sweet with the taste of

sitting down with someone who's looking out for me.

Aunty Em's grabbing at thoughts. Talking about me having something in my life to be passionate about. I'm thinking I got enough of that with Rhonda. I'm getting that Aunty's meaning something more than that.

'You gotta have something to commit to that's bigger than just you. It doesn't matter what it is. But you've got to find a way to just get out there and do it. What about your basketball? Maybe you could get a job down the gym, I don't know . . .' Aunty's got a way of talking round and about. Next minute she's worked her way right in close before you even saw her sneaking up. 'As long as you do something.'

I'm wanting to say yes, and I'll think of something, and I won't go balancing on no edges no more. I can't say nothing, but. I'm not knowing who the 'me' is that's gonna be doing it.

'I might sound like just another migaloo telling you what to do,' she says.

I'm looking at m'aunty. I forgot she was a whitefulla. She's my aunty. Don't she know that makes her one of us fullas?

'And maybe you think your uncle's not making much time for you. But maybe he's only just keeping his balance, too. He might look like he's got it all together but maybe he's down here, living a long way from where he wants to be, for some of the same reasons as you.'

That can't be right, I'm thinking. My uncle's a legend.

I'm wanting to lie down. Be on my own.

I'm thinking about Happy Valley. About lying out there, staring across at all my relations in the graveyard, that cement-ery. And how I was thinking I'd be headed over there, joining them under one of those tombstones.

Now I'm lying down here, staring across at a wall full of books. Dead people's thoughts. None of them my relations, I bet. I'm wondering, what the difference is from up there in Happy Valley to down here?

Maybe down here I'm on different land. It's not my land down here.

Different bed, maybe? This one's got sheets and a soft pillow. There's a hot and cold shower down here in Aunty and Uncle's flat.

No difference in here, but. In me. Inside of me, I come a long way to be back where I was, lying down, staring out at nothing.

☼

Rhonda comes home late. I've been busting to talk with her about the train and that. Somehow what I'm saying and what she's getting is two different things, but.

'I feel so sorry for your people,' she reckons.

I'm wanting her to see me. No Murri-fulla me, no this-fulla me, no that-fulla me . . . Just *me*. The fulla inside that's got no shape or size or colour. Just is.

'We've taken away everything you ever had. Your culture. Your Dreaming. Your land . . .' she keeps going on.

I'm getting gooli-up at her. 'I got my culture.' I'm standing my ground. 'Not all of it. Some, but. And m'uncle, he's got lots to give to me. Soon.'

She keeps calling me a Koori. I'm trying to explain I'm a Murri. Koori is what blackfullas down here call themselves. Up home, we're Murris. Some place else they got another name.

'Stop splitting hairs. You know what I mean,' she says.

I'm wanting to kick in a wall, break a window, do something that makes a difference. My words aren't working for me. I can't tell her how much her not knowing about us-fullas makes me feel like I don't exist. And her only seeing me as a blackfulla all the time, not just a fulla, makes me feel like I'm something else, not human.

'I'm not a kid.' I'm yelling. I'm not meaning that. I got no way of yelling about that other stuff, but. No-good, I'm grabbing any words to chuck at her to start a fight. 'You treat me like a kid.'

She punches back, no fists, but, just gooli-up words, same as mine. 'You treat me like an old woman.'

'Don't!' I'm angry.

'Do!' She's angry.

'You treat me like a weirdo pet lost its leg or something!' I'm pleased with that. I'm getting closer to saying something that could be true.

She's shouting big-time. 'I do not! You're the one that treats me like a freak!'

'Don't!' I'm yelling back.

'Why can't I come down the gym then? Watch the basketball? Why can we only muck around together when there's no one watching?'

I'm stuck. I got no answers.

I take off, back upstairs to Aunty and Uncle's flat, banging doors.

Later, she comes over. Says something about how we should cool it for a week. Me, stay over here. She, go visit some friends or an old aunt that's dying or something.

I'm laying down, staring up, thinking those Un-Happy Valley thoughts, my mind tied up into a tight ball, hard as a rock.

8

They can go those two, Uncle Garth and Aunty Em. Woke me up in the middle of this brown-black night, shadows from the streetlights playing games on the wall. I'm listening, trying to get my bearings, thinking I'm back at Rhonda's or down the Valley with all the arguing and fighting going on.

'Not yet, hear me?' That's m'uncle. He's a stash of dynamite. He can lay there quite happy and cop it sweet. Once that fuse is lit, but, you know he's gonna go off. Don't know just where and when.

'Explain to me why "not yet".' That's Aunty Em. She can make her voice go cold as. And that's only the tip of the iceberg. Before you know it, you're sinking, like the *Titanic*.

Uncle's on about something to do with keeping his head above water. How Aunty Em doesn't have to cop it every day in the face. He does. He doesn't even have to walk out the door and he's insulted, he reckons. For black-fulla's the insults start the minute you turn on the TV or pick up the newspaper or look at a carton of milk.

'It's all white!' Now he's gammin'.

Aunty's not laughing at that one, but. Not a good sign.

My uncle's solid when it comes to us Murri-fullas and how we feel. I'm listening up fully, wanting more.

'We have to cop your mob telling us mob what we think, feel, care about, want to have on our toast . . . what colour we like our knickers . . .'

Eh, good-go, I'm thinking!

Aunty's not budging. 'I'm not talking politics. Or knickers. I'm talking about your nephew!'

Hell! Did I hear that right? That's me. They're talking about me. They're fighting over me. I sit up.

'Being black *is* being political! We don't have a choice,' says Uncle.

'He needs you. Just get off your butt and take him with you out to a school for God's sake.'Aunty's pleading.

Uncle's staying cool. 'I'm not ready for him. And he's not ready for me.'

'That sounds good, but what does it mean?' Aunty's straight into him. 'You've got time for a hundred other school kids every day. Why can't you make space to take him with you, just once? You need him like he needs you. All you've got otherwise is work and sleep.'

I don't need to hear it. I can feel it. Uncle's about to explode.

'You know what sleep is to me? You ever bothered to ask? No. So I'll tell you. Sleep is the only place I can be human. The only place I don't have to deal with the crap of justifying what it is to be a blackfulla in this country everyday. My eyes are closed and it's just me and darkness. And that darkness, it don't scare me no more. I can be whatever I want to be and have no one standing there being my judge and jury. Sleep is the only place I can be a person, no labels attached. When I open up my eyes, I'm rested and ready for dealing with my anger again. And where does that anger come from? Dealing with crap like this. Justifying how it is I stay alive each day. It's a vicious circle and I'm getting bloody dizzy.'

I'm there with him, dizzy, like fully.

Uncle's not finished, but. 'And it's a fine balance. You mightn't appreciate how it is to have that balancing act going on each day of your life and not blow your top. And you're asking me to take him out to the schools with me? He's all over the place! He's gotta fix up his attitude first.'

Now I'm getting gooli-up. Stuff that! I'm not a mess. Well, maybe I am. I'm not thinking m'uncle's seeing that, but. I'm wanting to go in there and stick it up both of them. How do they know what I'm on about?

Aunty's talking up some more, but. I got m'ear to the wall. 'How can he get the right attitude when there's nothing to get an attitude about? Except taking drugs and sleeping with the woman downstairs!'

Hell! If I wasn't black I'd be red. Drugs? Me and Rhonda? Aunty wants Uncle Garth to have a talk to me about Rhonda. Shame job! I'm gonna die!

Uncle reckons I've got to make m'own mistakes and

learn from them. I'm with him on this one.

'We're responsible for him. We've got to make sure he's got something in his life to live for.' Aunty keeps at it. I'm with her. M'aunty, she's deadly.

Uncle's bringing in the big guns now. He reckons he had to earn the right to be passed on stories and to learn how to dance, how to paint up. He had to fight hard to earn the right to be given what's left of his culture. He says it's been abused, cut up, sliced and diced every which way.

'I mightn't have initiation scars across my chest but they're in here, across my heart! He,' he's talking about me, 'can't expect to rock up here and get it handed to him on a plate.'

'Is that your way of teaching him or just your cop-out way of dodging your responsibilities?' I wouldn't go there, Aunty, true god.

The fuse is lit. I'm blocking m'ears. But I'm opening them again 'cause that's me in there they're busting-up on.

Aunty's backing down. 'Well, I'll leave it to you. You speak to him. You're the Murri. You're his uncle. I'm just a migaloo.'

'Crap. You're part of this family. Who's dodging their responsibilities now, eh? He relies on you. You're his aunty. Anyway, Rhonda's one of you lot. You speak to her. I'm a blackfulla. That stuff's whitewomen's business.'

They keep on arguing. What's men's business, what's women's business, which one is everybody's business . . .

What's being black, what's being white, what's being human . . .

Now Aunty's cursing at the clock. She's gotta get to sleep 'cause she's gotta get up. She's real gooli-up that she's gonna be tired in the morning.

Uncle says stuff being tired. Stuff the time.

Aunty says, 'Stuff you!'

I'm laying back saying nothing, awake for the rest of the night.

☼

Since the train station, Aunty's been hugging me lots. When she leaves of a morning. When she comes home of a night. She checks on me before she goes this morning. I'm pretending I'm still fast asleep. She goes on out.

Uncle's off next. I still got m'head under the pillow. I wait till I hear that front door slam, then get up.

I'm cold in bed alone. I got used to snuggling up to someone warm and soft. I'm wanting to be downstairs. Down there where day is night and night is day and you can pretend there's no tomorrow.

I stumble round the kitchen for some food. Take it out the back steps.

The morning's bright as. I never remembered the day could be so bright. Rhonda'll still be sleeping, somewhere. I remember me trying to explain to her what sunrises look like up home. That sun coming up over the great long horizon, golden light, round ball of fire cruisin' up over the sea. She reckoned, 'You mean there's two parts to the day? A morning *and* an evening? I thought there was just evening.' I'm wishing I was back there with her and 2 Quack and their munyard ways.

My cereal tastes like cardboard. I can't make it go down. I put the bowl over to one side for later. Lay back and let that sun take me in its arms. The sun, just me and the sun, keeping me alive.

Laying back here, I'm getting a good look at m'self. Seems I got bits of me going in all directions. I can't get my mind to stay inside my head. I'm jigging about even when I'm supposed to be slack as.

I sit up. I'm still jigging.

There's something moving at the bottom of the steps. Down there on the cement. A speck, some little thing, looks like me, jigging around in circles on the one spot. I'm making my way down the steps. Closer I get, I'm seeing it's alive. Something struggling with what's hanging on to it, holding it down. Trying to wriggle out of its cocoon.

I'm watching the poor little fulla, that chrysalis there, busting his guts to get out of that hard shell. I can't take my eyes off 'im. He don't look like he's gonna make it.

That shell's real tough. Won't get off. He's all limp and floppy. A butterfly, I reckon. Could be.

I get a twig. Hold one side of the cocoon with it, real gentle. Then, slowly, lightly, with my finger and thumb, try to open out the hole where he's pushing the most. I'm feeling that little fulla struggle, then give up, struggle some more, then go quiet.

'I'm with you, little brother. Don't worry. I'll help you. I'll get you out, bro'.'

I peel the hard bits back. Got it. He's out. Saved the little fulla. I give him a nudge, gentle as. He lays there, but. No life in him. Not yet. I'm crouching down, blowing the softest breeze on his wings. He's gotta get up. He's gotta get those wings going and fly. With each breath I'm willing him to fly.

No-more, he don't.

Something warm and wet trickles down m'face. I'm wondering where those tears are coming from. I'm feeling naked, stripped bare of everything I was ever thinking I was. Maybe I'm not dead, but.

I'm feeling sorry. Real sorry. For that little fulla. For my clumsy hands. For not knowing which way to go, or where I am, or what I can do. Sorry for me, whoever that may be.

We're laying here, me and that dead could-have-been butterfly. The sun gone out on both of us, gone down behind some building.

I'm hearing that voice, that one I've been thinking is

teasing me and I'm not understanding. Real distant. I give in trying to make out what she's saying, my girragundji. I'm giving in to the sound, without making nothing of the words. I'm just glad I can still hear something going on inside me.

Could be minutes, could be hours or days, I'm laying here.

When I come back to where I am, I'm knowing I've got a feeling for something. A feeling for sound or some meaning to words. Not so much words, but a feeling for a message that don't need no words.

It's only you . . .

I'm getting a feeling for taking one step back up the stairs.

. . . can save you . . .

If I can take one, might be I can take another.

It's only you can save you.

Might be I can choose to climb back up.

The next step I gotta take is to get my butt out of bed and be ready to face m'uncle. I got it in me to lay it out straight with him.

Aunty Em shuffles out of the bedroom first, puts her rubber mat out in the lounge. Starts that stretching.

Me and this time of day, we're still strangers. I'm rubbing m'eyes, watching m'Aunty Em down on the floor, twisting herself around in a knot. That morning light's hugging round her bare arms, soft, cradling her into the day.

I flop on the couch, stretching out, hoping she might ask me to join her while there's no one watching. She don't seem to notice my thoughts. Keeps on going about her business, one position into the next.

It's me that decides to ask. 'Can you show me how to do that?'

'What, yoga?'

'Whatever?'

'Sure. Take your socks off first.'

'It's cold, but.'

'It's your choice.'

I take m'socks off.

I got m'head down and m'moyu up doing that dog-pose, feeling like a goose, all m'muscles yelling at me to get back on the couch. That's when Uncle comes past. Wouldn't you know it? I lay out flat on the ground, gammin' I'm resting, been sleeping there all night. He don't seem to notice if I'm moyu-up or moyu-down, he keeps on a steady course to the shower.

I wait till he's dressed, gets a bowl of cereal, milk and sugar, and's sitting down taking his time.

'I'm really wanting you to teach me dances.' I blurt it out, trying to be casual.

Something's fluttering inside me. I'm struggling with the words, tough as shrugging off a cocoon.

'To go with you to some schools.'

He don't seem to have heard me. I'm standing my ground, but, knowing one puff of wind could blow me over.

Then he looks up at me, into me.

Then he looks back down into his bowl of Weet-Bix.

'You be up and ready Monday, after the weekend.' I'm not that sure whether he's talking to the Weet-Bix or me. 'Tomorrow I wanna see you down the courts first.'

He washes his bowl, grabs his bags and heads out the front door.

Me, I'm standing there, not knowing whether I should be jumping for joy or running like crazy the other direction. It's one thing to be wanting something real bad. A whole other thing to get it and have to live up to having it.

Today, I got my work cut out for me, down the Pavilion doing work-outs, getting ready for the brothers.

☼

I got the rock in my hand. I let it fly. It hits the bottom of the net, making that swish-sweet sound of leather sweeping through nylon. That sound all shooters dream about.

I'm in! Me! I'm number nine to get a basket. Means I'm in the second team playing the first mob. Uncle shot one just ahead of me. We're on the same team.

'Yo, man.' I high-five Leaping Leroy.

He's on our team. Listen to me. 'Our' team like I was born part of it.

'I'll give you "yo".' My uncle mutters under his breath. He don't let me get away with nothing.

No matter, but. I'm in.

I start running all over the court. I'm going where space is, so I don't clutter everything up and get in no one's way. I reckon I'm doing great, finding a rhythm, blocking out, eye on the ball . . . Trouble is, the game hasn't started yet. People are watching me like I gone wongy. And I have!

The brothers make their way onto the court. Best shooter from each team shoots. First to get a hoop, that team starts with the ball. Leaping Leroy gets it for us. And we're away.

I'm getting into the flow, getting my rhythm, cutting

through the key, getting bumped, yelled at by m'uncle. He's coming at me from all directions.

'Get your feet set.'

'You're shooting like the Leaning Tower of Pisa.'

'Tuck your elbow in.'

'Follow through.'

'Block out!'

'Seal your man off!'

'Go to space.'

Space? Feels like I'm in outta space, some two-headed alien or somethin'. I'm trying to shove all this stuff in my head, what he's yelling out, and still keep playing basketball. I thought we were on the same team. Even my opponents aren't bagging me this much. I'm wishing I'd been doing some more training.

Richie Rich, he's on the other team. They're ahead. Leaping Leroy, on our team, he's going off.

'No, man, no, man . . . nooo! That was a foul, man.'

'Man, no one even touched you!' Richie's serving it back up to him.

'So, nigger, you saying that ball just jumped out of my hands? It's got a mind of its own, right? You expecting Leaping Leroy to believe that, man?' Leroy walks away disgusted. 'Hands foul, man. Our ball.'

People are coming from all around the gym to listen

to these fullas talk their talk. And I'm right there in the middle, part of everything. This is awesome.

Richie's on a fast break, with the ball, and with a load on his mind he's looking to be dumpin' off. He's steaming down the court. He's got the rock in his hand heading straight for the hoop with dunk in his eyes. I'm the only one standing between him and two points. I hear m'uncle yelling.

'Stay set. Stay set. Don't move.'

I'm thinking that's okay for him. He's in that safe place, trailing behind Richie. Me, I'm in that other place. That front-of-train place. That place you can't say nothing from.

I stay set to take the charge.

It's too late to run and hide.

M'uncle's yelling again.

'What?' I look over.

Next thing I hit the floor, flat on my back, this great big knee stuck in my chest, sucking the wind out of me. I can't breathe. His knee feels like part of my body. There's no room for air to get in even if it wanted to. I'm gonna die! Like fully!

'Yo, boy, yo . . .' Voices swirl overhead.

'You ain't gonna die on us, are you man?'

'He not gonna die. He's the man!'

'Hey, kid, you're the man.'

I can hear Richie in there. 'He d'man! Took it straight up.'

I may be a man, I'm thinking. I'm not sure I'm *the* man, but.

The brothers crowd around me, picking me up.

I hear Uncle Garth somewhere there. 'He done good.'

There's a lot of yo-ing going on.

Leaping Leroy takes over. 'He'll do all right, man. He got the stuff inside to make it in the game. Didn't back down. Took the hit and he's still alive.' He's got everyone listening. 'But it's our ball.'

He charges out onto the court. The brothers are back in the swing.

I'm trying to keep up. I'm weak. M'knees have given out. I'm feeling sick in the stomach.

Uncle cruises up beside me. 'Good on you, m'boy. You're learning. Sometimes you've got to put yourself on the line.'

After, I'm sitting there panting up big.

Leroy slaps me on the back. 'You're phatt man, phatt.'

No one's ever been calling me fat before. I'm too bony to be fat!

Uncle translates. 'That means you're cool. Phatt means cool.'

The Guru takes a seat next to me. Starts talking half-way through a sentence like we've been having this talk all along. He could be telling it to anybody, his shoelaces, or the basketball at his feet. He's talking, but. And I reckon

I'm the one that's listening.

He tells me these Saturday afternoons are more than what they seem. I'm ready to agree.

'The brothers, they're the ones that know,' he reckons, 'if you make it in here, you can make it anywhere. So, they don't go easy. They give it to you tough, man, because out in the world there you gonna need to know you can take it tough and still get up and play the game. That's why they're called the brothers. They're watching out for you.

'Maybe you could look at being a point-guard. I'm starting to think you might just have the mind-set for that. You gotta have courage, like the courage to go into the belly of the beast and find out the weakness. You think you got that kind of courage?'

I'm looking lame.

'I can see in your eyes you been to some of those dark places I been. You know what tough is. You might look shy, but inside there you've had to fight to stay alive, right?'

He's not holding up nothing for my answer.

'Where I come from, New York, you gotta get down and get dirty to survive. You gotta learn to walk round with your chest puffed out, never back off. You don't, you die. That gives you the courage to be a point-guard. Get it? No L.A. pretty boy's gonna be satisfied dishing off the ball so their team-mates can look good when they make an easy bucket. You gotta be prepared to sacrifice your own scoring when you're a point-guard. You gotta keep your cool in the middle of a riot out there.'

I'm nodding. Getting it. I think.

'I can see that in you. You got the heart to be a point-guard.'

I'm not knowing which way to look, like fully. I'm just looking straight ahead.

'You're gonna make it, man.' He's nodding, looking down at his laces. 'Because you're choosing to make it, right?'

His laces aren't arguing. Me, same. He gathers everything up. When he's ready, the Guru walks off.

Every bit of me is aching on the way home. 'Cept my heart. It's full as.

Uncle's talking up. 'If those migaloos don't respect you for anything else, they have to respect you for being faster and more agile than anyone else on the court . . . basketball, football, running . . . don't matter what it is. We're all equal when it comes to going for the ball or the finish line. It's only the best wins, no matter about colour.'

Sunday night I can't get that feeling for going to sleep. I wander downstairs. Rhonda's light's on. I'm thinking, gotta be more than a week's gone by.

I knock on the door. She sneaks a look through. Takes the chain off the lock.

'Hello, nephew.' Could be that first day we met, her soft voice floating across to me.

She's got her glasses on. Reckons she's busy studying. Says she's ready for a break and do I want a drink?

We sit out the back. Drink some cordial. She has a smoke. 2 Quack stays on the couch watching TV.

I tell her that I'm gonna be going out with m'uncle to a school in the morning. I'm gonna have to dance, like Murri-fulla dance.

'You better get a good night's sleep then,' she smirks.

I agree.

She gives me a kiss on the forehead and walks me to the front door.

I climb back up the stairs, m'mind running back over what's changed between us and the good old days . . . or nights . . . or days that were nights. I get to the top of the stairs and remember . . . I think I just called her aunty then when I said goodbye. No-good, Aunty Rhonda?

Maybe she's not my jalbu no more. Not like under-the-doona kind of jalbu. More like friend for swapping stories or talking about what's goin' down.

Or more like . . . Aunty! Good-go!

This smile rushes across m'face, tripping me up the stairs.

9

Not much room in here in the boys' toilets. Not for me and m'uncle and all our gear. Funky boys smells're thickening up the air, true.

I'm asking m'uncle if I can leave m'clothes on.

'Why?'

'I'm too shame.' I admit right up front.

M'uncle just grins.

I'm thinking I'm not ready for this. This painting up. And painting up's not ready for me. I'm not a traditional kind of blackfulla. I know I'm black as, as in the colour of m'skin. I'm wondering how deep that black goes, but.

'Here, put this on.' Uncle throws a bit of cloth at me. 'We gotta get started. That there,' he's pointing at the scrap of material in my hand, 'that's your real ticket. That's what'll get you on that bus ride, the most important one. The one that takes you back to yourself.'

My mind's spinning, taking me out bush somewhere, long way from anyone, just me and m'uncle teaching me things, important things.

I take m'clothes off. Try working out which way to tie that scrap of material round me. We call 'im judda-jah. Dancers up home wear them. They look like they been born in their judda-jahs, but. Me? I try and get a look at myself in the mirror above the washbasin. I'm naked except for this little red thing covering m'boy's bits. I'm thinking no one better look up when I bend over.

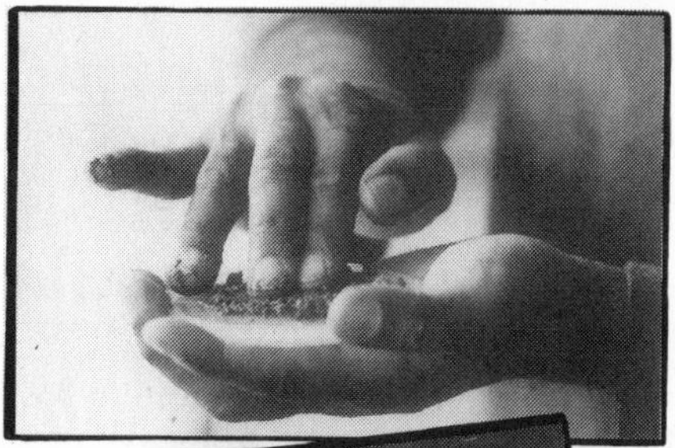

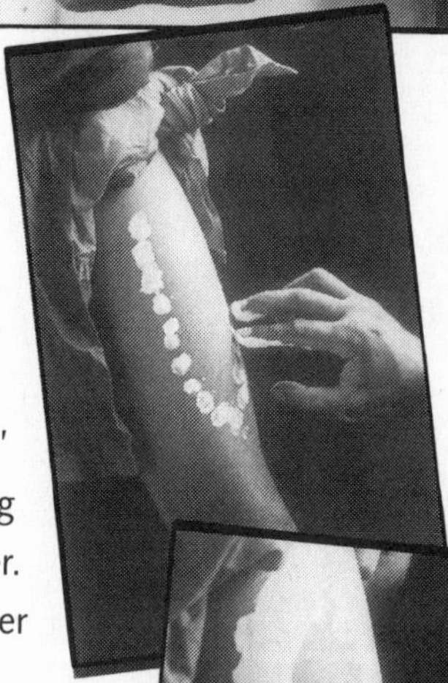

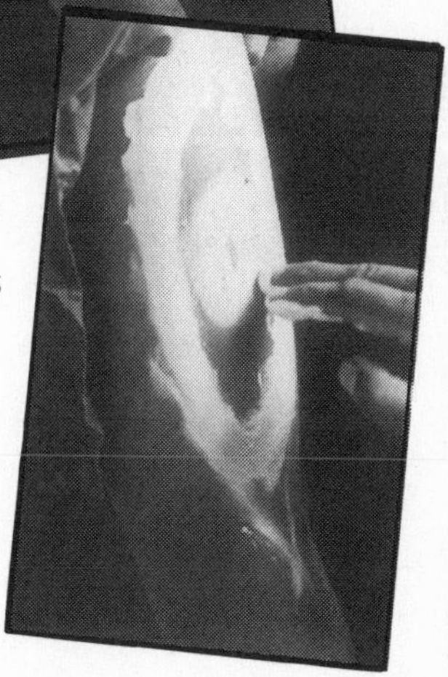

M'uncle takes the dry, powdery rock, the white ochre, and wets a bit on the lid of the container.

'This here, that's your mother.' He takes two of his fingers, drawing the wet paint over my skin. I shiver. Not from the cold. From the power of it, but.

'Mother earth from up home.'

He paints big butterfly wings in circles on m'thighs. Us fullas, Kunggandji mob, when we dance we shake our legs like imbala, the butterfly. I'm thinking of m'brother, that could-have-been butterfly, dying on the cement. He needed that struggle to make him strong enough to live. I didn't know that then.

Uncle smothers both palms of his hands in white ochre. Places them against my belly all the way up m'chest. The white hand prints of the ancestors holding me tight. He takes the yellow ochre and draws a rainbow up the middle. All the time he's talking, telling me things.

'Soon, you'll learn your own design from the old fullas up home. For now, you use this one here like mine.'

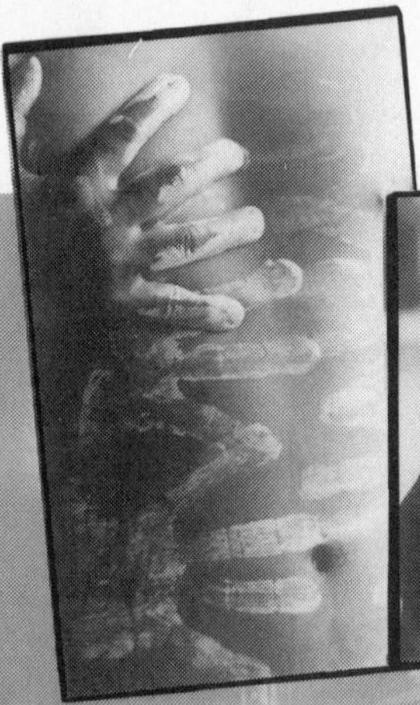

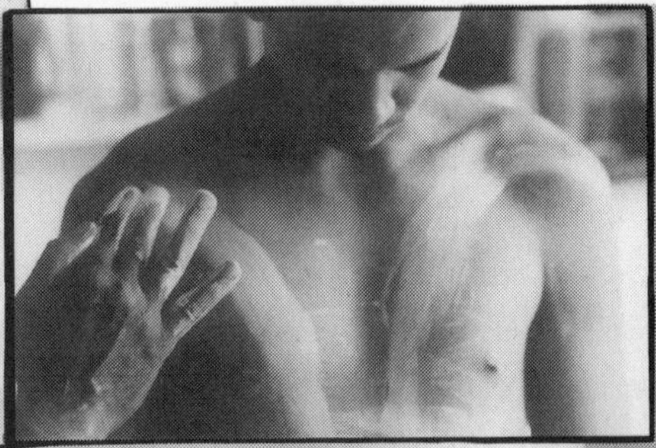

I'm trying to get a look at the new me in the tiny square of mirror. The fulla I see peering back out looks like he got a few thousand years of clothes on him. He's not naked no more. His mother earth is keeping him warm, shielding and protecting his spirit.

I've grown, true. I'll be the one ducking m'head under the basketball ring now.

'This yikki-yikki, he's magic fulla.' Uncle passes me his didjeridoo. 'When you play, you are its breath. This fulla here, he take your breath and he says things these fullas here never heard before. Takes them places they never been.'

My uncle, he sounds like one of those old fullas now. 'You'll meet people and have amazing stories to tell in your life because of this here, this magic stick, this yikki-yikki. Today, you do warrima, dance. Tomorrow, you start to play this here.'

There's a hundred sets of eyes're staring straight at me. Most of them never seen a blackfulla before, I bet. I never seen this blackfulla before, neither. Not dressed like this. My feet don't feel like they're touching the floor.

I stand off to one side, holding my uncle's yikki-yikki. Talk rustles round the hall of kids like they're leaves with a no-good wind shaking them up, making them wriggle and call out. Teachers're shooshing them.

My uncle, he takes control.

'Okay, everybody, give yourself a hug. Teachers too.'

Eh, look-out, everybody's hugging up, true.

'Then turn to the person next to you and give them a real big hug.'

That sends them off, rolling round the floor laughing and gammin' hugging and looking like they don't know what the hell's going on.

'No kissing. I didn't say anything about kissing!'

Now everyone's pushing and shoving each other, trying to get away. The whole place is alive. They got the message this could be fun.

Now Uncle gets serious, his voice strong and deep.

'I hope the spirits of the land that we are on today welcome me and my stories, songs and dances. Us fullas,' he's talking about me too, now, 'we're Bummah Murri. Bummah means people. Murri means from our area up home, up north Queensland. This fulla here, my nephew and me, we Kunggandji. You say that now. Kunggandji.'

Big mob of kids call out our name. Sends shivers up m'spine.

Uncle carries on. 'We're saltwater people 'cause we're on the coast. Aboriginal people inland there, they're freshwater people.'

I look around. Everyone's listening. No fulla's moving, or chucking off at what m'uncle's got to say, or nothing.

'A lot of people think us blackfullas are all the same, but we're not. There are about five hundred groups across the country with about two hundred and fifty different languages, and that's not counting all the dialects. We don't all speak the same, do the same dances, tell the same stories, sing the same songs. We don't all play this magic stick here, either.'

If they think Uncle Garth's real deadly from his talking, they heard nothing yet. Wait till he starts to play that yikki-yikki. He starts up, the drone settling the whole hall, closing us in tight.

The kids go real quiet, drawn into the sound, sucked into that hollow stick, and then into the air, way back somewhere. Me too, I'm in there, same. Don't know where I'm going but it's somewhere good.

Now Uncle Garth's talking about respect for all that's living and breathing. Plants, trees, the whole lot. He's telling about the crocodile and the boy that didn't listen. He's telling the kids if you don't listen properly you become lost and the only things that will find you are the bad things. In this story, it's the crocodile.

'The crocodile, he can be many things. He's even here today outside the school in your neighbourhood.'

Kids go all big-eyed. 'Where?'

Looking around the room. 'We've never seen crocodiles around here.'

Asking each other. 'Crocodiles down here?'

'If you listen properly, you'll never get to see him. You see, in this dance, this boy he never listened properly and he died. He got eaten up by the crocodile.'

'Wow!' The kids are in the palm of his hand, hanging on every word.

'He wears lots of disguises, this fulla crocodile. Could be drugs, could be alcohol, could be the big truck going down the road you don't see. He knocks into you, hurts you. Knowing what you're supposed to do and where you're supposed to be by listening properly means you never have to face that crocodile.'

I'm the wide-eyed one now.

'You don't listen, we got a name we call you. Binna-gurri. Binna, this one here,' Uncle's pulling his ear, 'means ear. Gurri means nothing in there. We call this boy that don't listen, Binna-gurri, deaf. Well, he's not really deaf, he can hear. But he only hears what he wants to hear not what he's supposed to.'

Uncle turns to me. 'My nephew here, he's going to play the boy, okay? And me, I'll be that crocodile.'

Uncle's grinning up at me. He knows there's no way out for me but to play being that boy. I'm thinking, he's thinking I won't be needing to act.

He's asking the kids, 'Guess who wins?'

The kids are yelling out, 'The crocodile!' Stamping their feet, clapping their hands, whistling.

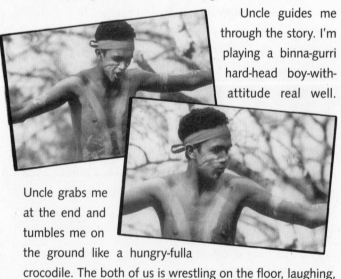

Uncle guides me through the story. I'm playing a binna-gurri hard-head boy-with-attitude real well.

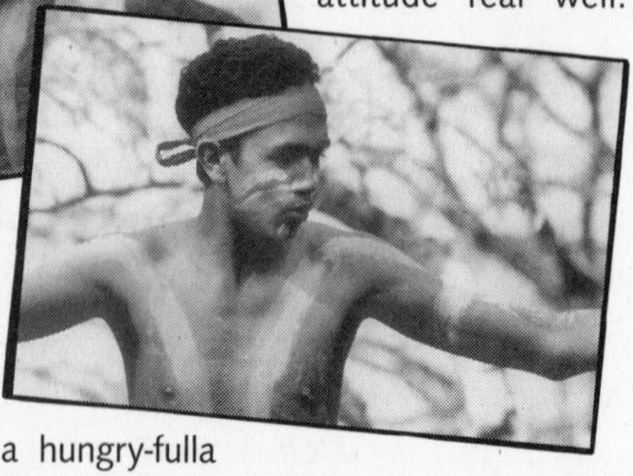

Uncle grabs me at the end and tumbles me on the ground like a hungry-fulla crocodile. The both of us is wrestling on the floor, laughing, shiakking, knowing that binna-gurri boy don't need to follow me no more. He can stay back there in the story.

Then Uncle, as the crocodile, and me as the boy, jump up and dance together, warrima, shake-a-leg. Shows respect of crocodile for boy, and same, the boy's respect for crocodile.

Uncle gets a group of kids to have a go at doing the Crocodile Dance. They go wongy, grabbing each other, eating each other up.

Then the whole mob of us is up there dancing. Seems we only started the performance. Already we're up to the last dance, but. Migaloo kids all around, dancing. Me learning along with the rest of them. We're doing shake-a-leg, kite hawk, kangaroo, goanna, crocodile . . .

Those imbala wings carry me back home. The home deep inside, no matter where I am. I'm feeling my cheeks damp with tears. I'm leaving them be, not wanting the warrima to ever stop. I'm hearing my girragundji voice chanting those old words to the songs. I'm happy just to be hearing.

I don't know when Uncle stopped clapping those boomerangs. Sometime I musta sat down with the rest of them. Part of me stays out there, dancing, but.

Then I hear this little voice next to me. I feel this tugging at my red cloth, pulling me back to where I am. I open m'eyes and look down. I'm back in the classroom, next to this little fulla tugging on m'judda-jah.

'Psst, psst.' He's smiling up at me. 'You just got this one piece on, eh?'

I look down. His bungy next to him's got his hand over his mouth giggling.

'Got any jocks on?'

'Ah . . . no . . .' I shake m'head.

'Well, how do you stop everything from flopping out?'

The boy next to him is bursting his sides, rolling round the floor, giggling. 'Don't ask him that!'

'But I want to. I want to know how he stops everything from escaping.'

I make up something about it being secret men's business how that all works. They go all wide-eyed wishing they had some of those kind of secrets.

After, kids're wanting my autograph. I haven't even played in the NBA yet! Lot of kids want to know about stuff to do with my culture. They ask me some things I never even heard of. If they were asking me about three-pointers I'd feel on safer ground.

'Are you a traditional Aboriginal?'

'Have you been initiated?'

I'm slow with my answering. 'Yeah . . . sort of . . .' Not! 'I can't tell you how 'cause it's sacred.' Gammin'!

They ask me what the drawings on the didjeridoo are. What the gecko means to my people? Is it my totem?

Things I don't know, I keep telling them are sacred so

I can get me some space to think. Same time, I'm laughing up. My Aunty Lillian, she paints real good. She painted this stick, this yikki-yikki of Uncle's. Beautiful geckos all over it. Truth is, she hates geckos. Curses them doing goona all over her nice, clean bathroom.

These migaloo fullas seem to think you can't paint a kangaroo without it meaning something. Sometimes, those Story creatures, their story's real sacred, for teaching you what you need to do. Sometimes, but, kangaroo is just a kangaroo.

One red-haired kid asks me to speak my language. Others join in. 'Yeah, say something, like "hello".'

My heart's hurting. I'm trying to scrounge round for some words. I'm trying not to go dry in the mouth, panic, or want to hit out at who it was took my words away. I'm wanting to be sitting down with those old fullas. Asking if there's any language left for me to learn.

Little girl, she's holding m'hand real tight, helping me through. She looks up, big eyes, voice thin as a whisp of smoke coming off a small camp fire. 'How long you been black?'

I'm looking up at m'uncle. He's laughing, listening for my reply.

'I reckon I was born black.' I'm looking back down into that fire burning in her eyes. 'I'm glad you asked me that, but, 'cause I reckon it's taken me a long while, maybe right up till now, to know that.'

That little girl gives me a long hard look, checking to see if I'm gammin' or not. I'm not. Then her look turns wise and old. She nods like she understands the lot of it and more.

Teachers ask us along to the staffroom. They're making cups of tea, waiting on us, asking how many sugars.

'Standard Murri-fulla,' I say. 'Milk and two, thanks.'

One teacher's telling Uncle Garth her whole family history, trying to find where she fits with it, like Uncle's got the lost map. Uncle's got that look on his face like he needs to find a big shady tree to lay down under and sleep. I'm there with him. There's a lot to take in for one morning.

The head teacher sees us out to the front door. Little fulla with a big heart. He's thanking us for what we've given to the kids and the teachers. I'm thinking he's meaning Uncle.

'And you too, young man.' He shakes my hand. 'You've given these kids a lot. They obviously loved you.'

'I loved them,' I hear myself say, not knowing where those words came from.

Back in the car, we don't talk. I'm not even thinking how flash I'm looking, paint still on, sunnies, and cruisin' in the Merc. More I'm sorting through the treasures I got in my heart. All the things the kids were asking. I'm not sure what I might have given them. I know what they've given me, but. They've given me back a part of myself.

10

By the end of the week, we've done about five more shows. All over Sydney. Little kids, big kids, even teenagers as old as me. Each time I get surer of myself, stronger at knowing my place, backing up m'uncle. He even got me introducing dances, telling some of the stories. I'm hearing m'voice little and squeaky at first, then getting stronger.

Friday night, Aunty Em's gone out on the town with a mob of teachers. Uncle and I are doing the dishes, laughing about all the different kids we met. Some of the questions them fullas asked and some of the things they did were real wongy.

One little girl, she wanted to know, 'Was Captain Cook a nice bloke?'

Eh, look-out, my uncle's not that old, I'm thinking.

Uncle reckons, 'I should have told her me and the Captain used to hang out up the Cape, fishing. We decided to name that place Cooktown after him 'cause he was such a nice fulla. Like us Murris never had names for places till them whitefullas come along!'

Then we get laughing about this little blackfulla at one school. Grade Six. I'm looking at myself and I'm thinking I'm pretty black. But this fulla, he was blue-black. My uncle started explaining the Honey Dance, the dance about searching for honey. That native bee don't sting, see. When that European bee come along, the one that stings, that jarred us Murri-fullas up.

Uncle needed someone to play his brother in the Honey Dance, and another fulla to be the tree. Uncle picked out this blue-black blackfulla. No-good, when that fulla come out, he stood up and looked m'uncle in the face.

'You're a racist,' he said. 'You only picked me 'cause I'm black.' He had a real grumpy face too.

'I jarred him up real good, but,' Uncle's reckons. 'I told him, "No I didn't. I picked you 'cause you was talking to your bungy there and you weren't listening to the story I was telling. You binna-gurri, in one ear out the other. Now you gotta listen up 'cause you gotta *be* the story." Did you see him, eh? See his face looking at me all serious, grumbling. "Well, that's okay then."'

Uncle yakais real loud, 'Can't be that easy!'

Washing up water's flying all directions. Uncle's cacking himself. I'm twirling the tea towel in the air, shiakking.

Uncle sits me down at the table, serious now. He's wiped and polished it till you can see your own face. He goes and gets his wallet. Doesn't say nothing. Just starts placing fifty dollar notes down in front of me. Six of them. All in a row. Three hundred bucks.

My eyes are big as full moons, watching.

'No, leave 'im.'

No way I'm about to touch 'im, that junga.

'Keep having a good hard look. That's yours there. You earned it.'

'Eh, look-out.' That takes m'breath away that does. I earned all that? I'm looking up at Uncle, make sure he's not jiving me.

'But before you touch 'im, you remember all those people that fought really hard so you could have that now. Your mum and all your aunties and their aunties and uncles for long time.'

I'm thinking of them and I'm thanking them and I'm listening to my uncle.

'See, that's how it is now. We can earn whitefullas' gold using the power of blackfullas' stories. That's what we gotta do. You earned this money teaching about your culture. That culture's like medicine. It can heal you. It can heal all these other fullas living here now, not knowing where they belong. For healing, we need whitefullas to hear about our culture. We need whitefullas to heal first so that we can heal. We gotta keep these stories going if we gonna keep ourselves alive.'

'Thanks, Uncle. Thanks for teaching me everything you know.'

My uncle grins. 'No, boy, I'm teaching you everything *you* know. There's a difference.'

The kettle boils. Uncle makes us a cuppa, proper tea-leaves in a pot. We settle into the couch, dunking biscuits, sipping sweet tea, lapping up that quiet between us.

'There's a lot more to learn. And it's the same for me too.'

We get back to talking b'ball, laughing about the brothers down the court, remembering how Leaping Leroy goes off and Richie Rich stirs him real bad. My uncle reckons he never seen no one go off at the Guru, but.

'I know it's only a game but if you love it with your heart it loves you back and will take you to many safe places on your journey.'

I'm feeling like I'm m'uncle's son, knowing he's enjoying having someone to yarn up to. And I'm feeling like he's m'dad I miss.

'I know there's lots of razzamatazz about wearing your hat backwards, and trash talk, and big money for those that make it. That's what lots of kids love best about it, especially you. That's what makes it fun. For me, I reckon you probably call that the window-dressing.'

We both stretch out now, feet up. We could be laying back home on the beach with the stars above and all night to shoot the breeze.

'You look at that American coach, Phil Jackson. He's a winner, eh?'

'Reckon!'

'When he was playing, he won a championship, then he goes on and coaches the greatest basketballer of all time, the mighty Michael Jordan, and takes him and his team to two three-peats – two times they won three-in-a-row championship rings.

'Then the coach continues on his journey with the L.A. Lakers, Shack O'Neil and Coby Bryant. And goes back to back. Two more championships. Now people are asking, how can this man do all this in amongst the glitz and glamour and money? How can he see through the window with all that window-dressing? You know how he does that?'

'Cause he's smart, I'm thinking. 'Cause he works hard? 'Cause he was good at school? 'Cause he trained hard, put in two hundred percent and never slacked off?

I'm grabbing at answers, all the ones I'm thinking I should be thinking. I'm saying nothing, but, 'cause to tell you the truth, I don't know.

Uncle Garth keeps on a roll. 'Phil, he goes back to basics, to the original people of the land he's in. The Lakota, American Indians. He uses the first people's wisdom for survival.'

I'm seeing the gleam of pride in m'uncle's eye and I'm feeling it too. I'm imagining us mob and the secrets we've got.

'And he works with all the other teachings that have

come his way. Yoga, that same stuff Aunty Em does, meditation, and he tells stories he's been given and teachings he's been taught. He listens and learns from many people to bring greatness and togetherness to the court, and make basketball players not only become winners of the game but winners in life.'

I never was thinking that stuff my popeye, my gran-dad, and my aunties are always wanting to teach me about the old ways could help me be a great play-maker on a basketball court.

'All I can say is, those teachings are something money can't buy.' Uncle's voice has gone all smoky, dust kicking up from those old-fulla feet stamping into the ground behind each word. 'Work on yourself first. Put yourself in the right state of mind, then good things will find you.'

I don't remember when our talking stops and that bed comes and carries me off to sleep.

☼

I'm waking with the first light poking into me through the curtains. It's the weekend. I got plenty of time to hang out here in Aunty Em's study and think on things. No way I'm sleeping, but. Dozing . . . dreaming . . . but not sleeping. I'm seeing kite hawks soaring overhead, I'm hearing the drone of the yikki-yikki, I'm flying through the air, dunkin', I'm sitting with the sun on m'face. I'm taking my time.

I'm knowing I've been through my initiation. Not traditional way, but modern-day initiation.

That morning light gets me up. I can't lay back no more. I'm full up with things I'm wanting to do.

I get that blank sheet of paper. The one I folded up beside the sofa that first day I was in Aunty and Uncle's flat on m'own. I couldn't find what it was I had to write back then.

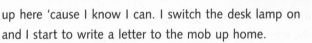

I take that piece of empty paper out and sit up at Aunty Emma's desk. I'm careful with all her stuff. But I sit up here 'cause I know I can. I switch the desk lamp on and I start to write a letter to the mob up home.

I done at least three pages before I'm even halfway through what I want to tell all those fullas about what's happening. What I'm getting m'mind set on doing. Telling them about the brothers, and what the kids at school ask. Something about m'friend Rhonda. Like about computers.

When I finish, I tuck in three of those fifties. I imagine those fullas eyes when they open it up and that junga falls out. The first fifty is for m'mum. The next for m'Aunty Milly. And the last is for m'sis. The one that brought the ticket down Happy Valley for me that day. I seen the look in her eye. I owe her this and more. I'll be sending lots more, I know that.

I sit back and look at that envelope, all addressed up. I reckon I'm gonna ask Rhonda to teach me some graphics on the computer so I can make my own designs and that. Like on letters . . . maybe t-shirts . . . deadly, eh? . . . or CD covers . . . Maybe they teach that stuff at Aunty Em's school . . . Maybe . . .

Next thing, Aunty Em's staring down at me with a cup of tea. Eh, look-out. I've been falling back to sleep. Deep sleep when that darkness is smooth and good to you, taking away your troubles. Not that jagged sleep, tosses you about with nightmares. That sleep I had then was the best sleep ever, like fully.

Aunty Em's sweet tea is waking me up, bringing me into the day. It's middle of the morning.

Aunty's about to go shopping with Uncle Garth. She asks me if I want anything special.

'Yeah.' I'm hardly recognising that steady, sure voice of mine. 'To come tell some of my stories to your class?'

She stands there, looking at me.

I'm taking another sip of m'tea, leaving my words out there for her to dodge or do what she likes with.

'I reckon we could fit that in sometime,' she says quietly.

I can tell that means 'yes'.

'Might get Uncle Garth to drive us, though. No trains, okay?' she smiles, only gammin', jarring me up. I didn't know we could be joking about that yet.

I'm working out how I'm gonna start my session. I reckon I'll stand up there, same as Uncle, m'two feet firmly on the ground, acknowledging the fullas from this place here, from this land, then telling them about my saltwater place where I come from . . .

And I'll be talking about what it's like for me. Telling my story of growing up around the mangroves, of hunting and fishing, aunties and uncles, of getting into trouble and getting myself out of it. Maybe, I'll even tell them about my girragundji, that voice inside me. Maybe . . .

There's a rhythm coming to my days. And m'nights, they're smoothing out. I'm drifting off to sleep, no worries about getting stuck halfway, waking up wanting to do some damage. That voice, that girragundji voice, it's quiet. It's there, but. As much a part of me as breathing.

I'm sleeping to the music of those old-fulla words didjeridooing me through the night. Something to do with feet. Something to do with having your feet on the ground. I'm not worrying about what I get and what I don't get. I'm trusting I'll be understanding when I need to understand. I'm just laying back listening till that sun lifts me out of bed. And then I'm just getting one foot to go in front of the other, on solid ground.

I'm waking, hearing Aunty Milly laughing up big. She's been watching for me, true, I know that.

I reckon I'll've saved up enough junga by the end of

the year to go back home for Christmas. I'll be getting that up-home dirt under my toenails. Aunty Milly reckons it's important to get that dirt in your feet. Makes sure you never forget who you are and which way is home.

I can see Aunty Milly looking up into that sky, watching for me there. Not for the moon, or for the stars. I'm no moon-face, good-go! And I'm no star yet, neither. I hear her laughing, but. She can see me clear as.

'Njunjul,' I'm hearing her calling out. 'Yibulla, Njunjul the Sun.'

Now she's laughing with me, and me with her. Njunjul means sun, see. The sun. My name. I've had that name since I've been a baby, warmed over the fire by my Aunty Milly. That's been our way of welcoming babies into the world. All the old fullas, sitting around the fire, saying the name for that newborn fulla.

I've not been using that name, but. Not for long time. Too shame. I could never spell it in migaloo school, see. And if I spelt it, they could never say it right. Me, I've had lots of other names. Some names I been called you wouldn't wanna know about, neither. Now, but, I'm taking on that Njunjul name, my name, that back-home name from the place I been born. That fulla Njunjul's been there for me all along, like fully. Only me, I've not been seeing that. Now I gotta be there for him. I'm feeling that warrior sun come to me.

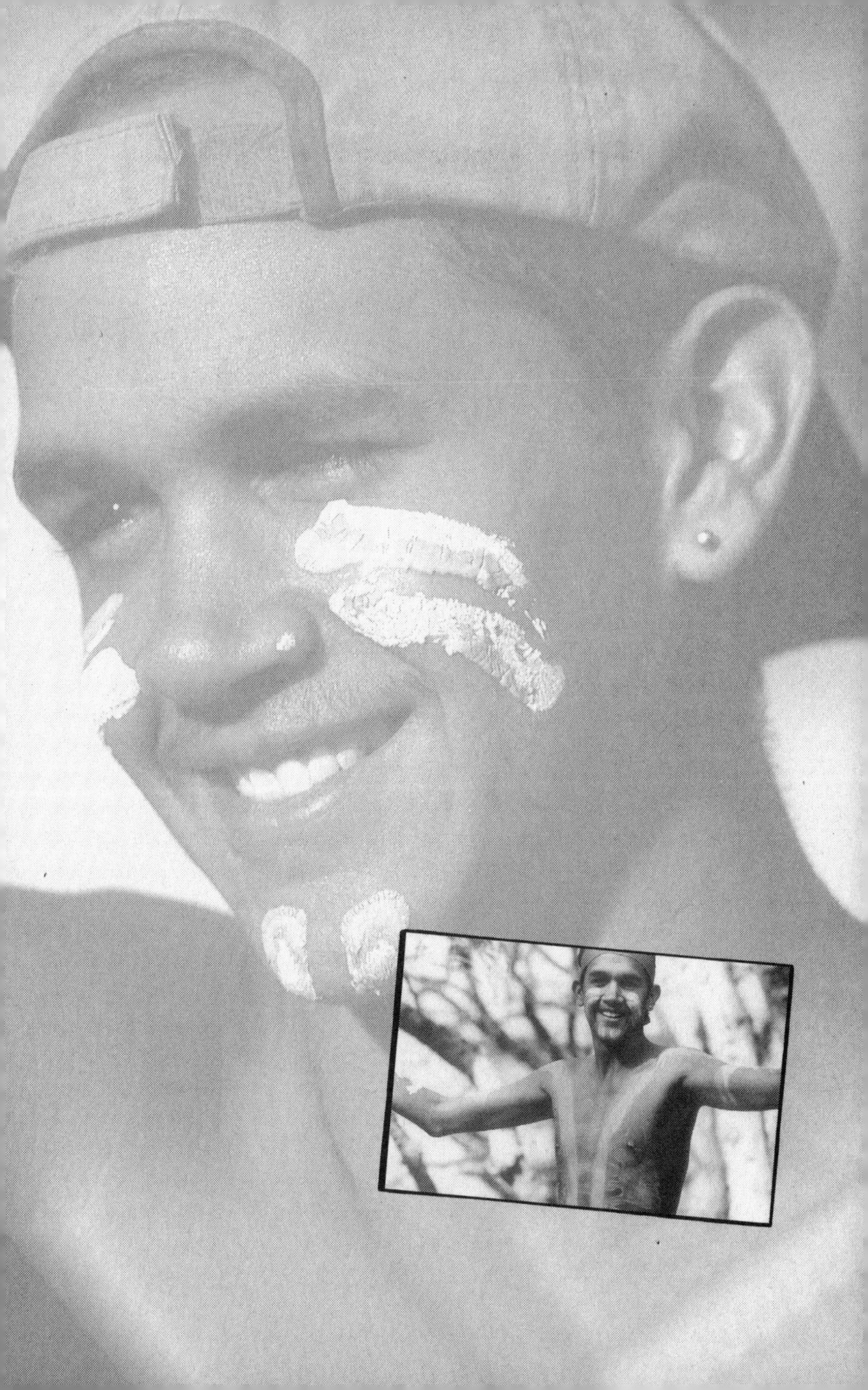

glossary of terms

binna-gurri	deaf, don't listen
boodgie	fart
bulleyman	policeman
Bummah	people
bungy	friend
fulla	fellow
gammin'	joking
gooli-up	angry
goona	poo
gulmra	dunny
imbala	butterfly
jalbu	woman
judda-jah	pants for dancing
junga	money
Koori	Aboriginal person from regions in New South Wales and northern Victoria

migaloo	white person
moyu	bottom
munyard	idiot, crazy
Murri	Aboriginal person from regions in Queensland
myall	person from the country
njarndi	marijuana
warrima	dance
wichay	which way
wongy	silly, stupid
yakai	call out, shout
yibulla	you fulla
yikki-yikki	didjeridoo

acknowledgements

'Njunjul' means 'sun' in Kunggandji language. It was the name given by the elders to Paul Pryor, Boori's brother. In writing this book Paul seemed very close in spirit. We offer *Njunjul the Sun* in his memory; and also in memory of Aunty Milda and Uncle Peter and days down Happy Valley; and in memory of Rhondda Johnson for the fullness of her life.

We give thanks to family and friends who have given so much to creating the characters of this book. In particular, we thank the elders, Aunty Val Stanley and Dot and Monty Pryor, Boori's mother and father, for their loving guidance; Chicky Pryor for making us laugh and cry; cousins Lillian and Gerry Fourmile for their help with all things including language.

Nicky Bidju Pryor has been photographed as the boy for *My Girragundji*, *The Binna Binna Man* and now this book. Not only do we thank him for his patience and trust, but also for the inspiration he has been in many other ways. Thanks go to Joe and Grace Lovell, Ciaran Ward, Paulani Winitani, and to the many nieces

and nephews who – some knowingly, some to their surprise – have inspired this story.

Thanks to 'the brothers', in particular Larry Holmes for sharing his knowledge of life and the game, to Richie Wedderburn for it all being good, and to Terell Domonique Jackson for giving his love (that's 'L-O-V-E, man').

And thanks to Karina Paine for being so generous in time and spirit, and John Douglas for offering his wonderful photograph of 2 Quack.

Thank you to the Happy Valley mob who made us welcome in their place: Delly Summers, Delly Walsh, Vincent Scott, Lucy Summers, Jody Langdon, Betsy Dalachy, Anthony Doolan, Arthur Langlo, Fred Langlo, Clarence Wyles, Monica Pichler and Les Brady.

And thanks to those who helped out with photographs at the Laura Festival: Rod North and Sons Coaches for their bus and Darryl Bray, the driver; David and Krysten Pawsey, Susan Ball, Peter Turnbull and Chris Grummet. And to Farren Karyuka, from Mornington Island Dance Group, for the last minute loan of a much sought after dusty red cap.

To Currambena Primary School staff and students a big thank you for making anything possible on a cold winters day. And thanks to Tempey High Language School – a centre for excellence in multi-cultural education – for permission to photograph.

And thank you to those who are always there with their insights and advice: Jenny Darling and Jacinta DiMase, our